A Contemporary Australian Romance

Forgotten

LENA WEST

Gymea Publishing

Published by Gymea Publishing

https://www.facebook.com/LenaWestAuthor/

www.lenawestauthor.com

ISBN-13: 978-0-6482671-7-1

Disclaimer

This story is a work of fiction.

Names, characters, places and incidents are the product of the author's imagination and are used fictitiously. Any resemblance to events, locales or actual persons, living or dead, is entirely coincidental. Some liberties have been taken and any mistakes are all my own.

Some actual locations may be referenced in passing.

Table of Contents

Here is Your Preview of

FORGOTTEN

Dedication

To Donna, a great sister-in-law who would make a fantastic publicist. Thank you for promoting my books among your friends.

FORGOTTEN

1

"Oof!"

David Curtis made a valiant attempt to maintain his balance, but with his crutches flying off in two different directions, his ignominious descent to the pavement was a forgone conclusion. Oblivious to all else, he lay absolutely still – taking inventory. Feet – check. Leg – check, protected by the moonboot. Hips – check. Arms, hands and wrists – check, check and check. Torso – check. He already knew he'd successfully protected his head, for what good that did him, the useless state his brain was in. Maybe a bang on the skull would have jolted the missing pieces back into place.

Anyway, it seemed he was still in one piece and good to go. Cautiously he levered himself into a sitting position, only then becoming aware of the young woman reaching down to help him.

A very pretty woman whose sun-streaked blonde hair brushed his shoulder as she reached down to him, ocean-blue eyes shadowed with concern.

The same woman he'd almost brought crashing down with him. A very pregnant woman, he observed. By rights, *he* ought to be offering *her* his assistance. His present helplessness galled him unbearably, especially in moments like this when it reduced him to feeling somewhat less than a man.

"Oh my God!" The shocked exclamation drew his attention away from himself. Drew his eyes to the woman's face.

"I know you!"

The words burst from his mouth before he knew they were there. He stared, struggling to remember the owner of those warm blue eyes and pretty face.

"David! Oh, God, David! Have I hurt you? Here, let me help you up."

"You know who I am! You recognise me!"

This discovery shocked him as deeply as his incomplete flash recognition of her had done.

"No. I'm not hurt," he answered, almost an afterthought. "That is, I'm not any more mangled than I already was. Are you okay? I haven't done you any harm, have I?"

Warily, he eyed the baby bulge which was almost level with his eyes. Hard to miss.

Krista Mallory snapped out of the near-trancelike state the sight of him had induced, and began busily retrieving his crutches.

"I'm fine, David. Meeting you here is a huge surprise, though. Last I heard, you were down in Concord."

Stop babbling, Krista, and help him up. You can't run off and leave a crippled man sprawled all over the footpath. Even if he is Captain David Bloody Curtis.

Even though her feet itched to take off in the opposite direction, she offered him her arm.

Between them, they got him back on his feet. Luckily, it was a manoeuvre his physiotherapist at Concord Repatriation General Hospital, anticipating just such an eventuality as today's fall, had made him practise over and over before letting him loose on his own.

Then the two of them stood there, staring at each other; each unsure what came next. A pair of jet fighters thundered across the Madonna-blue May sky, but neither of them, totally absorbed in their own mini drama being played out below, so much as glanced up.

"Well, as long as you're okay, David, I'll get going. I'm running late as it is, otherwise I guess I'd have seen you coming round the corner."

And run like Hell in the opposite direction, Krista added silently.

"Wait! Wait! You can't just disappear. Not when I've only just found you. You know who I am; and I recognised you, even if I can't for the life of me put a name to your face. I need you, Mrs …. At least tell me your name."

David clamped the crutch under his elbow and took hold of the woman's arm. No way was he letting her out of his sight till he could be sure of her cooperation. Or where to find her again, at the very least.

"I've got to go. I told you, I'm running late."

With a quick twist of her arm, Krista broke free and scurried through the door into the building next to where they were standing.

Making the best speed he was capable of, David swung into motion in her wake, blessing the automatic door which allowed him to enter on her heels. He caught up to her when, for the second time, she impatiently jabbed the button to summon the woefully slow lift. Another bonus for which he gave silent thanks. If she'd taken the stairs he'd have lost her.

Krista glared at him when he crowded into the small lift beside her, willing him to disappear. Even on crutches he towered over her, his upright carriage and dark short-back-and-sides screaming Army in a city where military personnel were thick on the ground. He might be temporarily disabled, but he was still every inch an officer, with all of that officer's natural arrogance.

"What's your name?" he asked again, his deceptively warm, chocolate-dark eyes drilling into her as they made their slow ascent.

"David Curtis, you know perfectly well who I am. What the Hell stupid game are you playing at?" Krista was furious.

With him.

With herself.

Making no effort at polite dissembling she added, "Whatever it is, I don't think it's very funny."

The lift ground to a halt, the door sliding open to release them from their enforced proximity.

"That's just it," David uttered through clenched teeth.

Why can't the damned woman simply answer my question?

Briefly, his temper rose to match hers. Until he drew in a deep, calming breath.

Gotta keep my cool, if I want her help.

Fixing his steady, commanding gaze on her, he grimly set about explaining himself, experiencing once again the self-loathing which invariably overpowered him each and every time he was forced to acknowledge his helplessness.

"When this happened," he gestured with his crutch, "I lost my memory. I don't even know who I am, except for what I've been told. My mind's a bloody blank. No name, no history, no friends I can recall, no home. Just a big, fat flaming nothing. You're the first person to stir so much as an inkling of memory, lady, and I'm warning you; I'm sticking to you like glue. I've got a gut feeling you can help me find myself."

Maybe she knows what unfinished, unrecalled business drew me back to Townsville.

David thought it, but no way was he sharing anything that personal. Not with anyone. Not even his psychologist; and Dr Henry Zelinka was privy to just about everything anyone knew of his past. He'd kept to himself the sense of burning urgency filling his mind when he first regained consciousness. A desperate need to return to Townsville to … To do what? One more thing he couldn't remember. However, broken in both body and mind, he'd lain there, tied to a hospital bed while his every instinct drove him to get himself to Townsville with all speed. Before it was too late.

Before what's too late?

The red-hot urgency faded in time, but never entirely left him. Using the ploy of returning to the last place he'd lived on Australian soil prior to being blown sky-high by a car bomb in a distant, foreign market place, he persuaded the Army to send him back here, eagerly anticipating a clearing of the mists fogging his brain. Then … Nothing. He'd begun to think it was all some jumbled figment of his imagination, cobbled together from the mish-mash of forgotten memories. Meaningless.

His flash of recognition when he'd seen this woman was proof he'd made the right decision.

Maybe, he cautioned himself.

Skidding to a halt, Krista turned to him, horror-struck.

"No memories at all? You really don't know who I am?"

"Really. Not a clue, except that for some reason you seem awfully familiar. Your knowing my name confirms you're someone from my past."

This cast the whole episode in a different light.

Krista chewed on her lip, caught between what she wanted to do, and what common decency demanded of her. Decency won out, but its victory came at a cost. She cast a longing glance along the corridor, *her* gut urging her to make a run for it. Shrugging her shoulders, she nodded at him to accompany her, moderating her speed to accommodate his slower dot-dash pace.

"I'm Krista Mallory." A quick sideways glance was enough to tell the name made no impact on him.

"I'll help you with your memories if I can, David, but right now, I really am running late for an appointment."

She shouldered open the door into the waiting room, expecting him to take a seat out in the corridor. Half-hoping he'd be gone when she emerged later on.

"Krista Mallory." She gave her name to the receptionist. "Sorry I'm a bit late. Parking is horrendous in this part of town."

"Not to worry, Ms Mallory. We're actually a bit behind schedule ourselves, today. I'll just let Samantha know you're waiting. Oh!" she looked up, smiling broadly. "You've brought Baby's Daddy with you. That's so nice."

Krista glared over her shoulder. That infuriating man had followed her in! Couldn't he take a damned hint and keep out of where he wasn't wanted? She turned back to set the receptionist straight, but was pipped at the post.

"No! No, you've got it all wrong. I'm not Baby's Daddy." David couldn't have sounded more horrified. "I'm just a friend of Ms Mallory's."

You're not even that! Not any more!

Krista felt an unreasonable rage boil up inside her, and tamped it down.

"Why don't you both take a seat till Sam's ready."

Sensing the tension in the air, the receptionist waved them to the half-dozen chairs ranged along the wall. Making a speedy escape through the interior door, she left them to sort out their differences.

"What is this place, anyway?"

David had followed Krista Mallory without looking to see where they were going. Now he looked about him. Except that the public information posters were mainly of babies *in utero*, it looked pretty much like a doctor's surgery. He'd seen enough of those in recent weeks to be a connoisseur.

"I'm here for an ultrasound check-up to make sure the baby's progressing according to plan." Krista picked up a three-month-old magazine and began flipping pages, ignoring the sensational headlines screaming celebrity scandals.

"Can I watch?" David recoiled from her fury as she dropped the magazine and swung to face him.

"What the Hell for, David? It's an ultrasound of *my* baby. How is that any business of yours?"

"It's not."

He'd asked impulsively, without thinking, only to realise he really did want in. Now he tried to come up with a reason which would make sense to Krista. To himself.

"It's just …" he began, then started over when the words came to him. "For months I've been shuttled back and forth between doctors and therapists and nurses and orthopaedic specialists and back again. All trying to mend what's broken. A baby … That's different. A baby isn't broken. It's perfect. It's hope for the future. A promise of good things ahead. Good times. I feel in need of a ray of hope after all the dark clouds surrounding me."

Krista blinked hard. Why did the damned man make refusing him so difficult? Then she thought of another reason he should be there during her scan, but this one she kept to herself.

One day it might be important to be able to remind him of her generosity if she let him see her baby today.

"I suppose it'll be okay."

She tried not to sound grudging, but wasn't sure how successful she was. Ignoring her reluctance, David smiled. A great, beaming smile that had her blinking madly again.

"Hi, I'm Sam. Samantha Reine, Ms Mallory. If you'd like to come in now?"

Krista levered herself out of the chair and headed over to the door leading through to where the procedure would be carried out. Behind her she heard a scuffle as David also rose to his feet.

"Er ... Sam? Do you think my friend here can come in with me?" Still reluctant, Krista crossed her fingers, hoping for a negative reply. No such luck.

"Why, sure. Most of our mums have someone with them holding their hand. This is a really special moment."

"Thanks Sam. David Curtis." Balancing on one crutch, David held his hand out.

"Been in the wars, there, David," Samantha commented, shaking his hand briskly. Not waiting for an answer, she led the way in, waving Krista to the couch and David to the chair near its head.

Literally, David thought, glad Sam had meant the question rhetorically and he wasn't forced to repeat the hated spiel yet again. Talking about the car-bomb which he couldn't recall always made him uncomfortable. He *ought* to be able to remember an event that had torn him, and his life, apart. His body was healing, but not his mind. Maybe it never would.

Uncomfortably averting his gaze from Krista Mallory's bulging, exposed tummy, he focused his attention on the screen, settling himself as comfortably as he could in the low chair.

"There we are." Sam played the wand over Krista's gel-slick abdomen. "There's our baby. Playing a bit coy today, turning his back on us. Hope you folks weren't counting on learning the gender."

While Sam did what she had to, Krista and David were both riveted to the screen, watching the baby floating gently in its small sea of amniotic fluid, arms waving and legs cycling, all in slow motion.

"Is he alright?" Krista whispered, totally rapt. She didn't even register when David, equally rapt, clasped her hand tightly in his. Didn't register her hand returning his grip with equal fervour.

"Sure he is. Absolutely perfect. Everything's normal for this stage in the pregnancy, Mother. You can stop worrying. Like what you're seeing here David?" Amanda, the receptionist, had warned Sam something was going on between this man and her patient, but to her mind he was no different to the hundreds of expectant fathers who'd sat in that chair before him.

"Umm." Then, without taking his eyes off the screen, David continued, his voice low and wistful. "I never got to see my baby like this. My fiancée aborted him without telling me."

Gaping, Krista exchanged a silent look with Sam then turned her head to study David's face. His concentration still fully taken up by what he was watching on the screen, he hadn't registered his words.

Krista struggled to remain silent, her mind reeling.

For a man with amnesia, she marvelled, *that was a pretty big incident to recall, and, from the look on his face, I'll bet he doesn't even know it happened. He never said a word about either a fiancée or a baby before.*

If she'd had her wits about her back then, she'd have seen his failure to talk about himself, about his past, as a symptom of his lack of commitment to their burgeoning relationship. But no, she'd been stupid. Blinded by lust and a handsome face into believing herself in love.

Love! Hah!

Bitterness for what might have been, tinged her thoughts, after which, she found it hard to pay attention to her baby. She felt almost as confused and uncertain as she had the day of her first scan, although for a different reason. Then she'd still been undecided about whether she was even going to *have* the baby at all. Angry at having unsought single parenthood thrust upon her, termination had been a possibility she was seriously considering. She'd told no-one. Not Mum. Not even Lorna, her BFF. Just in case she decide against becoming a mother. My body; my decision, she told herself then. Even though she'd decided against an abortion, that was a principle she still firmly believed in.

Not until she'd seen those tiny, tiny limbs waving to her from the screen and heard the strong, rapid beat of the tiny heart did she fully accept that it was an actual baby growing inside her. A baby! Not some abstract theoretical possibility she could easily eliminate from her life. Tears had flooded her eyes, and she'd been lost.

Harder and faster than she'd fallen in love with the despicable rat who was her baby's father, she'd fallen in love with her baby. From that point there'd been no going back. No more dithering about whether or not she could do this.

She was having a baby. A real, honest-to-goodness baby. And it was hers. Hers alone. The rat wouldn't be getting a look in.

That night she'd called her parents and her friends. With every sharing of her news her commitment had grown stronger. Her confidence in her future as a single mum surer. If she could have wound back time, she wouldn't have done one thing to prevent her baby's conception. This was going to be the most loved and wanted baby in the history of unplanned pregnancies.

Krista tuned in once more to the present, where, ironically, David Curtis, the rat in person, was holding her hand, listening with her to the baby's strong, constant heartbeat. Her emotions a hopeless tangle, she wondered how quickly she could give him the slip. He had forfeited all right to a place in either her, or her baby's life. She wanted nothing to do with him. Nothing at all. Although …

That huge secret he'd let slip might have had something to do with his past attitude. Maybe …

Maybe, but she still wanted nothing to do with him. Although …

It seemed no time at all till, with ruthless efficiency, Sam shooed David out, helped Krista tidy up, and sent her back to the waiting room.

"Don't rush off," she said.

"I'll make you a copy of today's scan."

While they waited, Krista glanced up at David.

Noticing her quizzically raised brow, he snapped out of the thrall the sight of her baby had placed him in.

"Thanks, Krissy," he whispered, leaning forward to kiss her on the cheek, unwittingly landing yet another blow upon her already damaged heart.

Krissy!

Hearing the well-remembered pet name only he had ever used, almost reduced Krista to tears. She'd thought she had put David Curtis behind her, but the last hour had proved how persistent, and how fragile, her feelings for him still were.

David Curtis was unfinished business.

Should I tell him? she wondered, not entirely sure exactly what she meant, there were so many thoughts whirling around in her mind. Finally, she decided to confine her interactions with him to the help with his memory which he'd asked of her. Anything else carried with it the potential for unbearable pain when he remembered her properly, as he surely would. Probably sooner rather than later.

That was the second … no, the third time he's had a memory flash this afternoon, even though he's completely unaware of the last two.

Then Sam was back, with a copy of the scan for each of them. Voicing their thanks, Krista held the door open for David to manoeuvre his way through. Mulling over her dilemma, she slowly made her way out of the building.

"Hey, where are you going?"

Feet automatically turning towards the parking garage, Krista was lost in memories of her own. David's question dragged her reluctantly back to the present.

"You promised to help me," he reminded her. "I thought we could make a start over coffee."

Sharing more time with David Curtis today was the last thing Krista wanted, but he was persistent, his intractable stubbornness a trait she remembered well. It seemed he hadn't changed in that respect. Or in any other essential of his nature? A tiny shudder rippled up her spine. She'd do well to bear in mind the old adage regarding leopards and their inability to change their spots.

"Okay," she agreed, accepting defeat. She'd answer enough of his questions to satisfy him, then disappear; and that would be an end to it. Better to do it now than have another meeting with him hanging over her head.

"There's a nice little café I often visit when I'm in this part of town," she said, leading the way.

2

"So, David, what do you want to know?"

They had given their orders and no further procrastination was possible. Krista braced herself, then relaxed when his first question was one she could answer quite readily.

"How did we meet, Krista? Where? When?"

Well that's easy enough. So far. And she'd be sure to find a way out of answering if his questions cut closer to home.

"August last year. It was all to do with my work. I'm a writer, and I was doing research for the book I was working on at the time."

"A writer?" Krista's spine stiffened at the cynical tone, and she sat a little taller in her chair, preparing to defend herself.

"Yes. A writer. Three of my novels have been published, one also made into a movie. And, I've already sold the movie rights to my latest book which is due for release Easter next year. So you see, David, I'm sufficiently successful to be able to give up my day job to write full-time."

She didn't mention the handful of self-published short novels. No point in blowing her trumpet too loudly. He hadn't been impressed the first time, and didn't sound overly impressed now.

"You were doing research, you said?" Ignoring her claim to fame he doggedly pursued his own agenda.

"That's right. In that book one of my main protagonists is in the Australian Army, and I wanted to be sure I had my basic facts right. You know, military language, protocols, weaponry etc. I didn't want some reader tearing it to shreds because of a mistake I could have easily corrected with a little extra attention to detail." Krista glanced at the unimpressed male across the table, then shrugged and continued.

"That's why I applied to the Base Commander at the Lavarack Barracks here in Townsville for assistance. He delegated my request to Major Cynthia Wallace whose duties included public relations. She invited me out to the barracks for an interview, then handed me over to you."

"What was I expected to do? Couldn't they have given you a few brochures and let you watch a parade or two, then leave you to get on with it?"

How weird, Krista mused. *We had almost the same conversation when we first met. He was just as sceptical then, only he was constrained by his orders to render me 'all reasonable assistance'.*

"You weren't best pleased," she admitted, lips twitching in her effort not to laugh as she recalled the incident, "but orders being orders, you carried it out to the best of your ability."

She remembered his salute, stiff with outrage, when Major Cynthia Wallace reiterated her orders.

~~~~~

"Captain Curtis, I'll be holding you responsible for any misinformation or bad publicity the Army receives if you fail to adequately educate Ms Mallory in the way the Military does things. Let her shadow your unit for the next week, and arrange for her to interview some of your men, and whomsoever else she may wish to consult."

What David Curtis hadn't realised was that Cynthia Wallace, admitting to being a fan of Krista's, had stretched her own instructions to offer assistance to the very limit. It had been with a look of acute loathing that Captain Curtis had turned to Krista as they left Major Wallace's office.

"Come with me, Ms Mallory. I'll need to think how to go about this."

"Please, call me Krista," she had responded. "You know, Captain Curtis, it might be easiest all round if I just tag along with your unit, watching what's happening from the sidelines. I can talk to the men and ask my questions during their downtime. During meal breaks and the like?"

Struggling to keep up with his long strides, she offered him her best placatory smile.

He had hummed and hawed a little; male face-saving of a kind she was familiar with; but in the end, he agreed with her, as she'd been confident he would; adding a couple of stipulations of his own.

"You'll remain at the observation posts where I put you unless I invite you to do otherwise, and you'll obey my orders without question. If I tell you to do something, do it. We're not playing schoolyard games here. Some exercises are dangerous, especially if we're using live fire."

He stopped, turning to face her. Unsmiling, he waited till she halted beside him.

"Is that understood, Ms Mallory?"

"Understood, Captain Curtis. And the name's Krista."

"You're here to learn how the Army does things. You're not here to distract my men, so you'll be addressed the way they are, Mallory. Do you understand?"

"Yes, Sir! Should that be accompanied with a salute, Sir?"

Annoyed, she couldn't help answering defiantly.

"You're not one of my men, thank goodness, so we'll dispense with salutes."

All that, and he didn't even crack a smile.

Krista kept her lack of enthusiasm to herself. It seemed she'd better acquire a thick skin if she was to survive a week in this man's company. She hoped the rest of the unit were friendlier. Aware she was still under critical observation, she nodded her agreement.

"You're too distracting in that get-up. Come with me."

She looked down at her crisp navy suit and white blouse, wondering how he could possibly consider such bland, conservative clothes distracting. What did he expect her to wear, for God's sake?

Trailing after him, she climbed into the passenger seat of the modern version of the army jeep, and he drove off, weaving his way through the back streets of the base. Arriving at a parade ground where a troop of soldiers were drilling under the eagle-eye of their sergeant.

Standing beside the vehicle, they silently watched until the sergeant stood down the men, several of whom were actually women, Krista observed. Looking forward to getting a female perspective on the Army, she began compiling a mental list of gender-specific questions to ask them.

"Sergeant." Captain Curtis strode forward, Krista scurrying in his wake. "Meet Ms Krista Mallory who'll be joining us for the next week. Ms Mallory, Sergeant Brian Wilson. Sergeant, I'm making Ms Mallory your responsibility. Mallory, what I said about obeying orders applies equally to Sergeant Wilson. Co-operate, and just maybe we'll return you to civilian life in one piece."

"Pleased to meet you Sergeant Wilson." Krista offered her hand, and, to her surprise, had it shaken enthusiastically. Brian Wilson, about ten years Captain Curtis's senior, even smiled at her.

"You're the writer, aren't you Krista?" he said, holding on to her hand. "I recognise you from your photo on the back of your books. Kate, my wife, is a huge fan. She's going to be so jealous when I tell her I met you."

He finally released her, turning to his captain, the smile abruptly wiped from his face when he realised David Curtis didn't share his enthusiasm for their visitor.

Out of the corner of her eye Krista caught sight of curious glances and eager whispers being exchanged between the soldiers sprawled on the grass nearby. Maybe this research exercise wasn't going to be such a trial after all. Not if she kept her distance from Captain Curtis.

"Glad you know who Ms Mallory is, Brian. We're under orders to render her 'all possible assistance' in some research she's doing for an upcoming book. I'd appreciate any ideas you might have on how best to go about it."

"Joining us, you say, Sir?" Brian pushed his cap back, scratching his head. "Not just a few interviews, then?"

"No. Orders are she's to tag along."

The sergeant tugged his cloth hat into place, straightening to subject Krista to an impersonal scrutiny.

"Seems, to me, Sir, if she's joining us in the field for a week, she'd be better off dressed appropriately, don't you reckon?"

More criticism of her clothes! At least Brian Wilson wasn't calling her a distraction. Krista gave an almost inaudible sniff.

"Sorry Krista. Didn't mean to be rude, but ordinary clothes will be too fragile where we'll be going."

"It's okay Brian." Defiance led her to address the sergeant by his Christian name. "The captain has already pointed out that I'm dressed inappropriately."

Her remark earned her the officer's frowning attention. She thought for a moment he was going to comment, but he chose to ignore her beyond that single disparaging glance. A short discussion in which Krista was not invited to take part, ensued.

The outcome was that Krista would be kitted out in uniform, boots and various pieces of equipment deemed necessary

Suits me, *she shrugged. She didn't want to ruin any of her own clothes, anyway.*

"I'll arrange a room for you in the Officers' Mess. If you're late, we'll go without you, so you won't want to be driving in from wherever you live at the crack of dawn every day, and sometimes we don't finish up till quite late in the evening."

David Curtis had smiled grimly, causing her to believe he might be relishing her likely discomfit at being forced to rise so early. If so, he was going to be disappointed to discover she was an early-bird.

A few phone calls, and it was all arranged. Kim Lawrence, a bubbly, blonde corporal, had been detailed to take her to the Quartermaster's stores to collect her kit, then deliver her to the Officer's Mess with orders to settle in.

"Today's Thursday. I'll give you the weekend to free yourself up for the week. Report back Sunday night, ready to start Monday morning. You'll be given a schedule to study, and I'll collect you at four forty-five. Am. Don't keep me waiting."

"Yes Sir!"

It took an effort not to click her heels and throw him a mock salute, but nothing was to be gained by getting him off-side before they even started.

Further off-side, *she amended. He already appeared to have taken a dislike to her.*

~~~~~

Sipping her peppermint tea, Krista explained to David the arrangements he'd made to integrate her into his unit.

"As I said, you weren't best pleased with the assignment, but once committed, you didn't hold back in giving me what I needed for my research. For which I am very grateful, as the information I gathered from you and your men made a huge difference to the authenticity of my characters and their lives."

About to expand on that brief statement, Krista was interrupted when her phone began playing *Fur Elise*.

"Excuse me David. Lorna, what's up?" Krista stood, moving far enough away to ensue privacy.

David, about to chase after her again, relaxed. The monster hold-all she toted was still parked beside her chair. She'd be back.

When she was, she was in a rush to be gone.

"Sorry David, I know you're not finished with your questions, but I've got to go. My friend Lorna is held up by a bushfire that's cut the Bruce Highway just south of town. I've got to collect her kids off the school bus." She fished in her wallet for a business card. "Here. Ring this number in a couple of days and we can set up another meeting."

She was gone before he could struggle to his feet. He turned the card over in his hand. Not much on it beyond her photo, name, a mobile number and an email address. She might have said to call in a couple of days, but he reckoned he'd be calling a lot sooner than that. A spark of excitement lit up his insides. Finally, he could see a dim light kindling into being at the end of the tunnel.

He studied Krista's card again. Caught up in his personal quest, he hadn't given it much thought earlier, but Krista Mallory was a very attractive young woman. Smart, too, he thought, recalling the books she'd written.

Attractive, smart, and somebody else's woman, he reminded himself. That baby she was carrying had a father somewhere.

FORGOTTEN

3

"For God's sake, Kris! What's wrong with you? Why would you get involved with that bastard again after what he did to you?"

Exasperated, Lorna Jansen, short, sable hair lifting with the abrupt movement, flung her arms wide, almost dousing her friend with the glass of Jacob's Creek chardonnay she held.

"Oops!" She performed a small miracle, regaining control of the glass in time to save its contents. "But really, Kris! I'd have thought you'd know better."

"Oh, Lorna. Stop exaggerating. I'm not involved," Krista used finger parenthesis to emphasise the word, "at all. I explained. We met by accident." She took a half-hearted sip of pineapple juice from her own glass. "Gee I'll be glad when baby's born and I can have wine again."

"Hah!" Lorna giggled, brown eyes sparkling. "Don't forget you're planning to feed the darling little monster yourself," she reminded her friend. Speaking from personal experience, she added an extra caution.

"That's another few months of abstinence, you know." Another extravagantly relished mouthful to make her point, then Lorna doggedly returned to the contentious subject of David Curtis.

"Why didn't you simply walk away from him? He'd hardly be able to catch you on crutches, even though you have slowed down a bit in the last couple of months."

Krista frowned, squirming a little. She loved Lorna dearly, but sometimes she wished her friend was a little less opinionated.

"I almost did, only then he told me about his amnesia, and I recalled Kate Wilson saying something about it too, when I phoned her to see how Brian was. You know, the sergeant who was nice to me. He had a nasty gash from flying shrapnel when the car bomb detonated, but it was David with his leg smashed in three places, who bore the brunt of the explosion. He took a blow to the head and was in a coma for about a week, then woke up with amnesia. At the time, Kate said the doctors expected his memory to clear as his physical condition improved, so I hadn't given it another thought. Seems they were a bit off in their prognosis. Although ..."

Her voice trailed off.

About to tell Lorna about the amazing revelation David had made during the scan, she changed her mind. That had been both unwitting and deeply personal. Even with her antipathy towards him, she wouldn't subject David to the sort of speculation it would arouse. Still, she might ask Kate about the ex-fiancée next time she was on the phone to her.

"Although?" Lorna prompted.

"He almost recognised me. He said it was the first time he remembered anything at all. Maybe he is starting to come out of it. It hasn't really been all that long."

"All the more reason to steer clear of him."

"Maybe. We'll see how much he remembers."

"If he wants help with his memory, I could tell him a few things. Perhaps I ought to come with you when you see him again."

Krista screwed her mouth up in a moue of distaste.

"No thanks. It will be bad enough without you starting World War Three. I'll tell him the barest minimum, then get shot of him. At least I'll have time to prepare. Not like today. It was such a shock, Lorna. Bumping into someone, then seeing it was *him*."

~~~~~

Not long home from Lorna's, Krista was sitting down to a dinner of grilled barramundi and salad when the phone interrupted her. Hastily swallowing a mouthful, she answered rather testily. It had been a long, unsettling day. She was tired, just wanting to be left in peace to enjoy her meal.

"Yes?"

"Krista Mallory?" Krista groaned silently, recognising the voice she'd be hard put to forget.

"What do you want, David?"

"I know you said you couldn't see me for a couple of days, and that's fine, but I'd like to set it up now, if that's okay?"

"Hang on."

Of course the damned man wouldn't wait. He'd always been like that, wanting everything organised to the last detail; preferably yesterday. Amnesia or not, he hadn't changed much. Krista rummaged in her tote for her diary then sat and swallowed another succulent mouthful before picking her phone up again.

"Can't fit you in tomorrow," she muttered through another mouthful. "The next day okay? I've got a doctor's appointment in the morning, but we could have lunch together afterwards and work our way through your list of questions."

Because, she thought sarcastically, *he'll have a list for sure unless he's changed radically*.

The David Curtis she remembered was an inveterate list-maker. She'd once teased him mercilessly about this habit while secretly acknowledging it was actually reassuring to know he could be relied on not to forget anything important. A splutter of laughter at her unconscious mental pun turned into a coughing fit as she choked on a morsel of carrot

"Sorry," she murmured, knowing she ought not to make jokes like that at his expense, even if only in her own mind, but it was either find something to laugh about or sink into a fit of depression and end up drenching her pillow in tears. Something she'd sworn never to do again.

Unaware of the direction of Krista's thoughts, David answered calmly.

"Lunch. Day after tomorrow. That's Wednesday. Good for me. How about I pick up some food and we have a picnic on The Strand? After months in hospitals, I'm savouring being outside in this glorious weather."

"Fine. I'll meet you near the rock pool about eleven thirty. Bye David."

Abruptly breaking the connection, Krista hurriedly scribbled a note in her diary and turned back to a meal which didn't seem as appetising as it had mere moments ago.

Savagely scraping the remains of her salad into the compost bucket, she hoped it would rain on Wednesday.

~~~~~

It didn't rain on Wednesday. Naturally. The one reliable thing about the weather was its propensity to be the opposite of what one wanted.

"David! Over here!"

Standing, Krista waved her hands, calling out to attract his attention. Arriving first, she had staked out a shady bench with a pleasant view of the water. A seat and view she had shared with David Curtis several times in the past. She wouldn't draw attention to that fact, but maybe it would jog his memory.

"Krista." Unsmiling, David carefully lay his crutches down alongside the bench and slid the backpack to the ground before seating himself beside her.

"David, there's something I …"

"Krista, before we start, I want to …"

They both started speaking at the same time, their words overlapping each other's. With a self-conscious giggle, Krista indicated he should go first.

"Mine's not that important, David, and you're looking very serious, as if something is bothering you, so let's have it," she urged, when he would have given precedence to her.

"Well, okay. If you're sure."

She nodded emphatically.

"The thing is, I've being going over the other day in my mind, and I realised that actually, you didn't seem particularly thrilled to see me again."

Astute of him.

Lips curved into a grim smile, she nodded at him to continue.

"That flash of memory made me think we must have been friends. Good friends. Only in retrospect I'm not so sure. No-one I've spoken with has ever mentioned you, and your name isn't in my address book. I pushed you into talking to me, but if we're not friends, I don't have any right to expect you to help me. Tell me the truth, here, Krista Mallory. No polite lies for the poor cripple."

He determinedly maintained eye contact as Krista stared at him, her mind running at a hundred miles a minute. He'd just given her the perfect out.

So why wasn't she jumping at the chance to be shot of him immediately? Why was she even hesitating? Why couldn't she simply give him the answer he seemed to be expecting, then get up and walk away. Forever.

But she couldn't. Not when he looked so lost and alone. So miserably unhappy. She dropped her eyes, confused by her reluctance. Something inside her made it impossible to turn her back on David Curtis if there was even half a chance that …

That what?

Her mind shied away from giving itself an answer. Sighing, she re-arranged her jumbled thoughts and lifted her eyes to his again.

"Before I answer your question, David, I need to explain something. This morning while I was at my doctor's, I asked a few questions about amnesia." She saw David bristling with indignation and cut him off before he uttered a protest. "No names. No personal information. She thinks it's research for a book. She's often helped me out with medical questions, so she won't think twice about it."

She peeped sideways, relieved to see him settling back in his seat. Licking suddenly dry lips, she steeled herself to continue.

"I asked about memory flashes and how to answer the sort of questions you've got for me, David. It's not her field, but she was pretty sure memory flashes can be seen as signs that your memory is beginning to return, but it's not an exact science, so she said it would be impossible to offer a time-frame, or even the assurance of a full recovery. She pointed out to me that every case is different."

"I know all that already. I've been examined by a whole battery of neurologists and psychologists and all the rest, and they all say the same thing."

"No need to sound so impatient! You've had time to get used to it, but it's all new to me. Anyway, to get back to what I was saying, she reckons I need to be careful with the amount and type of information I give you. I should try not to overwhelm you with too much minutiae. Keep to the bare minimum of true facts and leave out the emotions and assumptions, etc."

David nodded slowly. His shrink had said something similar to him.

"No more than the basic who, what, where and when," Krista continued. "Otherwise I'll run the risk of contaminating your returning memories with my impressions of events. So that's what I'll do. You need to remember for yourself."

Dr Robards had unwittingly given her the perfect rationale for keeping anything she didn't want to share to herself. And that included almost everything of importance.

A stubborn look settled upon David's face, but he simply sat there beside her, lost in his own thoughts until she began to fidget, wondering if he was ever going to return to the present. Finally, he sighed. Flexing his shoulders, he turned to face her again.

"So, you still agree to help me, then? Even though you're not best pleased about it?"

Krista's jaw dropped. She'd forgotten his assumption that they might not be friends. Closing her mouth with a snap, she narrowed her eyes at him, wondering when she'd decided not to take advantage of the let-out he'd given her. Lorna would have words to say about her failure to effect her escape. Lots of words.

Maybe I won't tell her everything.

"Yes. I'll do what I can, David. As to our relationship, we got off to a rocky start, out at Lavarack, both of us jumping to conclusions about the other based on insufficient personal knowledge." She took a deep breath. This was where her story might come unstuck.

"As we got to know each other better, we came to respect each other, and yes, I suppose you could say we became friends. Unfortunately, we had a huge difference of opinion, just before you shipped out"

She was entering dangerous ground, and quickly backed off.

"We didn't have time to resolve it then, and I guess I was still a bit cheesed off with you when we met the other day."

Cheesed off! What a colossal understatement that is!

Krista squirmed in her seat, but forced herself to finish what she'd started.

"None of that is relevant now. You helped me research my book, so in return, I'll help you research your memories."

"I suppose no-one mentioned you because the ones who knew we were friends, or whatever, are all still overseas?"

"Guess so. What's first on your agenda?"

"I thought we could carry on from the other day. Tell me about the way your research project was carried out."

"Right, well."

~~~~~

Arriving at Lavarack Barracks late on Sunday night, Krista found the promised schedule for the coming week lying neatly in the very centre of her tiny desk. It had been amended with hand-written notes on what to wear, what to carry, etc, so she studied it carefully, determined not to give David Curtis reason to find fault with her.

Before going to bed, she set out the PT uniform Kim had requisitioned for her, filled her water bottle and set the alarm on her phone. She wanted these soldiers to take her seriously, and had a gut feeling it wasn't only David Curtis who'd be watching for her to fail to make the grade.

Let them watch!

There was no way she could ever pretend to be the equal of a trained soldier, but the morning run, at least, held no fears for her. She would do her best, openly acknowledge her weaknesses, and hope to earn their respect. Snuggling down in the strange bed, she prepared herself to get a good night's sleep. She'd need it.

Waiting in the designated meeting place, she was half-way through her warm-up stretches when David Curtis jogged down the stairs from his room.

"Good. Nice to see you understand punctuality."

He eyed her up and down, taking a visual inventory, unless, of course, he was simply admiring her figure. No. Uniform inspection it was. His next words proved it. "Those shoes aren't regulation issue."

"No, they're not. I've no intention of ruining my feet in running shoes, or boots, I haven't had time to break in. I crossed all footwear off the list you gave Kim Lawrence, and brought my own. I think you'll find them quite appropriate."

She stared him down, then, grinning to herself, fell into step with him as he silently nodded, conceding her the point, and led the way outside. After delivering her to Brian, he'd set off on his own run, making it clear he had no intention of baby-sitting her.

"Just try and run with us for a little way, then turn around and walk back, Krista. No-one expects you to be able to do a five-kilometre run."

About to explain herself, the sergeant's kind, but condescending words brought out the devil in her.

"How fast do you go, Brian?"

Krista smirked at his answer, then moved off with his squad.

She kept up easily on the run, but the rigorous drill program straight after with barely a break nearly did her in.

"Bit of a dark horse, aren't you Krista Mallory."

Looking up from the last of her cool-down stretches to see David Curtis standing beside her, she couldn't help her triumphant smile.

"I'm a fitness instructor," she explained. "Or I was till last month when I became a full-time writer. I've kept up my personal routines, which include a five-kilometre run before breakfast most days."

"You did well." His grudging praise brought a warm glow to her heart, especially when it was seconded more generously by Brian Wilson.

"Yeah, but these guys are way fitter and stronger," she acknowledged, speaking to the nearby audience as well as to David and Brian.

"I wouldn't have a hope of keeping up all day, if this is a typical beginning."

"You won't have to, today at least," David answered.

"After breakfast I'll be taking you on a tour of some of the specialised departments so you can get an overview of what an Army base is all about. We do more than keep fit, you know."

"Oh, I know," Krista agreed airily. "You learn to fire weapons and kill people as well."

That earned her one of his disapproving looks, but he didn't deign to comment, merely turning to lead the way back to shower and change for breakfast.

Recording his explanations on her phone as they toured the base, Krista thought she detected a gradual easing in David's attitude towards her. During lunch, she peppered him with questions, all of which he answered patiently. She even surprised a half-smile, quickly smothered, out of him with one of her pithy, irreverent observations.

At dinner that evening, an informal occasion on which she was permitted to wear her own civilian clothes, Major Cynthia Wallace joined them, wanting to hear how she was getting on.

"A-Okay, Major," she replied jauntily. "Captain Curtis is doing a great job of correcting my many misconceptions of military life. And, whoopee! I believe I'm even going to get to fire a gun tomorrow."

"Do I detect a disapproval of our purpose here, Krista? And I believe we can dispense with rank for the moment. Call me Cynthia."

"Sure, Cynthia. I guess that makes you David, Captain. And no, Cynthia. It's not the Army I don't like, or soldiers; it's the need to have an army at all. However, don't worry about me writing anything subversive."

Krista grinned at the consternation on both their faces.

"I'm realist enough to know the human race has a long way to go before we evolve to the point where nations no longer view each other aggressively. I'm really very grateful for your co-operation, since I do like to get my facts right. Also, I apologise for being a bit of a pain in the neck. I never have taken well to being regimented."

"And do you find Krista a pain in the neck, David?"

Cynthia's mouth curled up at the corners, as if she relished the chance to put her junior officer on the spot. Krista chuckled at his diplomatic answer.

"Ms Mallory …" Cynthia raised an eyebrow at his continued formality, so he began again. "Krista exaggerates. I've been pleasantly surprised at how well prepared she is. Certainly, my time has not been wasted with frivolous questions. She even showed a few of my men up this morning when she outran them. I predict they'll all be working much harder tomorrow so as not to be shown up again by a civilian. Especially a female civilian."

It feels nice, knowing I made a good impression on David, *Krista thought as sleep claimed her that night. It didn't even register with her that she was no longer thinking of the formidable Captain Curtis as anything other than 'David'.*

~~~~~

Keeping it as brief and impersonal as she could, Krista gave David a run-down of her first day at Lavarack Barracks while they consumed the salad rolls and cold drinks he had provided. His glum expression was enough for Krista to tell none of it had raised so much as a glimmer of hope.

Desperately, she tried to stir a hint of enthusiasm in him. David depressed and feeling hopeless tore at her heartstrings in a way a confidant, top-of-his-world David never could.

"I guess you can revisit all those places anytime you want to. See if they stir any memories, David."

He frowned at her, as if he didn't understand what she meant.

"You are living out at Lavarack, aren't you? You must have a ton of things there to help you remember."

"No. I was there at first, but although everything around me had a familiar feel to it, nothing clicked as a true memory."

He took another small bite, chewing reflectively.

"I left there last week. I've got a flat near my physio so I don't have to travel across the city every time I have an appointment. I had to leave anyway. They've given me a medical discharge, you know," he added, almost as an afterthought, although Krista was quite sure it wasn't.

She couldn't help a gasp. The Army was David's whole life. What would he do without it?

"The paperwork was delivered this morning."

Well, she guessed that went a long way to explaining his downer of a mood which had been bothering her since he'd arrived.

"I knew it was coming. The doctors are pretty sure I'll make a good recovery, physically, but this leg means I'll never be Army-fit again. So, I'm out." He glanced sideways, taking in her concern, but misunderstanding its cause.

"It's not all bad, you know. They're continuing to pick up the medical tab, and my pension means I can afford a roof over my head. Along with my savings, I'll be financially secure, even if I can't run to too many luxuries."

"So," Krista chose her words carefully, "do you have any plans for the future?"

She worried that he'd be feeling cut adrift.

Abandoned by the institution he'd once referred to as his family.

Maybe his amnesia would help to cushion the blow now, but sooner or later he'd remember. Then he'd feel the full brunt of being stripped of the career he loved.

No wonder his subconscious was holding back on remembering, when knowing and feeling might be worse than not knowing!

Poor David. Krista's heart flooded with tears she had difficulty holding in.

"Not yet. There's plenty of time." Hating the pity he saw in her face, David tried to sound more upbeat, and almost succeeded.

"First, I'll learn to walk without crutches or sticks, get my memory back if possible, then I'll look for something to do. I think I'd like some sort of small business where I'll be the boss. Maybe in the eco-tourism field."

That sounded more like the man she knew. Krista nodded to herself, making a snap decision she just knew Lorna was going to try and talk her out of.

Maybe she'd stick around and be David's friend. The old David had behaved unforgivably, but this man, wounded in body and mind, wasn't *that* man at all. Was he? So, it'd be okay to help him out, wouldn't it? It would be the humane thing to do. Until he didn't need her any more, or ...

But that was racing too far ahead.

"You know, David," she said, changing the subject. "I've been thinking about these memory-jogging talks. If you agree, I think they might work better if I take you to places I know you've been, outside Lavarack and the Army. You know, sight, sound and smell to give more cues."

David nodded slowly. What she suggested gelled with the advice he'd had from his therapist.

"With that in mind, would you like to go for a drink tomorrow evening? I'll answer a few more of your questions then, if you like?"

"Okay, but you know, Krissy, I'm beginning to think it's all a waste of time."

"Maybe. Maybe not. I've picked up on several small things you've said which you had no way of knowing unless you remembered them. I didn't mention them at the time because I didn't want to put pressure on you, but I found them encouraging."

"And I suppose you're not going to tell me now, either." He sounded thoroughly disgruntled.

"No, I'm not."

Ducking her head to hide her grin, Krista busied herself collecting the debris from their lunch.

A quick check, and she walked across the grass to deposit it in the nearest bin. When she returned, David had got himself onto his feet, crutches in place. He was staring around him, taking in the scene as if he'd never seen it before, even though he'd been sitting there for over an hour.

"This is a nice spot," he said, his voice dreamy and distant. "Hard to believe we're so close to the business district."

David stood there a while longer, saying nothing. Krista picked up her tote bag, preparing to leave. Suddenly, he spoke again, electrifying her.

"We swam here. In the rock pool."

He swung round to face her, moving so fast he almost lost one of his crutches. Krista reached out a hand to steady him, ending up clamped tightly against his chest.

His heart raced under her hand. He laughed, with tears streaming down his face at the same time. Krista couldn't help laughing with him.

"I remembered!" he shouted. "I remembered! You're a bloody miracle worker Krista Mallory."

She was still held against him, so closely they were almost nose to nose. Almost mouth to mouth. An intent, arrested look came into David's eyes, causing Krista to hold her breath as he lowered his mouth to hers in a searing kiss. An eon passed in seconds as her body remembered how it felt to be kissed by David Curtis.

Remembered, and responded.

Then he was holding her away from him. Disengaging from their embrace as if he'd been scalded.

A look of wary uncertainty crossed his face.

"Sorry. Sorry. Shouldn't have done that, only I felt so over the moon at finally remembering something I forgot myself."

Krista's giggle was dangerously close to hysteria.

"Sorry. Bad pun. I know you're involved with someone else, your baby's father, and I've got no right to be kissing you. I won't do it again. But it is good news, isn't it?" His voice rose exuberantly, his faux pas dismissed as he celebrated.

Krista ignored his reference to someone else in her life. For the time being she was content for him to believe that. It buffered her against becoming too deeply involved with him.

"The best news, David. It proves what I said a few minutes ago. How much do you remember?"

He frowned, delving into his mind.

"Not very much. Just swimming. Playing with a frisbee, I think. You were there, and others as well, but I can't see them clearly. That tree. Did I climb it? I feel as if I did. Is it a true memory, Krissy, or something my mind created from what I'm seeing here today?"

"A true memory, David." Krista hastened to allay his sudden anxiety. "One you can take to your psychologist. There were other people. Friends. It was a really hot day, and we came here to cool off as there was a shark warning for the beaches along Rowes Bay where we'd planned to swim. It was a happy day all round. We were playing, and the frisbee got caught in the tree. You climbed up to retrieve it."

If he wanted to know more, he'd have to remember it for himself.

She remembered though.

Remembered, and wished she could turn the clock back.

~~~~~

David had swung up into the small tree as if climbing was second nature to him. The other men had cheered him on, then, the frisbee returned to six-year-old Pete Jansen, who'd declared it his favourite birthday present, everyone else had run off down the park to continue the game.

Leaving Krista laughing up at David who was still perched on a low branch.

"Join me Krissy." David's invitation, accompanied by a grin which drew her eyes to those delectable lips she'd been dreaming of ever since she'd tasted them on Friday night, set Krista laughing.

"No! No way. My speciality is falling out of trees. I'll keep my feet on the ground, thank you very much, Captain Curtis."

"Oh, come on, Krissy. I dare you. I won't let you fall. Some fitness expert you are, if you let a little tree get the better of you," he scoffed.

No chicken, Krista looked from David to the tree, and back again, considering. It was such a little tree, surely she wouldn't fall. Not if David was true to his word.

"Okay. I'll do it! Give me a hand here David. Just till I'm on the first branch."

Obligingly, he leaned down, wrapping one strong, sinewy hand around hers, hoisting her up.

Going up was easy. Even distracted as she was by David's hands sliding over her ribs and around her waist as he guided her to a safe perch.

"See? Nothing to it. I reckon such a brave trooper deserves a reward."

David's husky, low voice set butterflies dancing in Krista's belly. When he lowered his head he moved slowly, gauging her reaction to the offered intimacy. Her lips parted automatically, her senses leaping in anticipation, as he zeroed in on his target.

On Friday night he'd plundered. Today he teased, brushing his lips across hers so lightly they barely touched. Krista leaned forward, silently demanding more.

"Hey! You two lovebirds up the tree! It's time to cut the cake."

"Come on down Auntie Kris. Watch me blow all the candles out and get my wish."

Sighing, Krista drew back, feeling for the foothold on the lower branch. She might have braved a bit of adult heckling, but no way was she setting a bad example in front of the kids. The leaves rustled loudly as she pushed them aside, so she couldn't swear to it, but she thought there had been an answering sigh from David before he slipped past her to help her down to the ground.

"We'll take this back to your place after the party," David whispered, his warm breath tickling her ear. Taking her hand, he raced her back to the party site.

"Were you kissing Uncle David?"

Krista looked down at the birthday girl, Pete's twin sister, who'd sidled up beside her, claiming her free hand in a sticky paw.

"Nooo Jilly. We were just climbing the tree."

True, as far as it went, Krista rationalised, her heart slowing from the rapid thunder of a minute earlier. But she couldn't help smiling at David's promise for later. Or was it a threat? A promise, she decided. Definitely a promise.

~~~~~

Krista blinked frantically, stemming tears as she recalled the happiness of that day.

Leading the way, she settled her sunglasses firmly in place to hide her eyes, and set off across the grass to her car. Clicking the doors open, Krista slung her bag onto the back seat.

"Can I give you a lift, David? You can show me where you live, then I'll know where to pick you up tomorrow evening."

"Why not? I don't live very far from here. I had a really lucky break. I was just walking down the street when I saw the owner of the apartments hanging out a vacancy sign. He had just finished repainting after the last tenant moved out not long ago. Letting me have it on the spot saved advertising for a new tenant." He frowned. "It was actually a bit odd," he added pensively. "He didn't even ask for references, but I didn't care. It saved me a lot of bother, too."

Krista moved the passenger seat way back to accommodate David's extra inches and gammy leg.

Deceptively roomy though it was, a Honda Jazz wasn't made for lanky cripples. Not that he'd be a cripple forever, of course.

As David directed her to his apartment, Krista began to get a hollow feeling in the pit of her stomach. They couldn't be going where she thought they were? Could they? Sure enough, they not only came to a stop in front of the Reef Gardens Apartments, but when David invited her in, he led the way across the courtyard to number five.

"Here we are. As I said, I was really lucky to get this. Ground floor so it's easy access on crutches, and the pool's just over there. A bonus, since the physio recommends I swim every day. There's two bedrooms, so I've turned the second one into a mini gym."

He flung open the door, waving her in, his mood now buoyantly optimistic.

"What do you think, Krissy? As soon as I saw it I got a happy feeling, as if I'd found a place I could call home. Do you like the furniture? It just seemed right, when I saw it in the shop."

He rattled on, not waiting for an answer.

Just as well. Krista was too stunned to give one.

He'd even furnished her old apartment in almost identical style to the way she'd had it, except for the gym. She'd used the second bedroom of number five, Reef Gardens Apartments, as a study. She wondered why Sam Leong, the landlord, hadn't said anything.

Surely he must have recognised David? Before she could ask, David had provided her with an answer.

"The landlord gave me a funny look when I told him I had amnesia as well as a gammy leg. Hope he doesn't think I'm the kind of nut case who'll be a nuisance to the other tenants."

Question answered.

"Shouldn't think so. Sam Leong doesn't say much, but he's pretty cluey. I'll have a word with him if you like."

"You know my landlord?" David swung round, surprise. all over his face.

"I went to school with his daughter." True, as far as it went, even though not the whole truth. Krista laughed at David's incredulity.

"Townsville is a big city, but a lot of the older families like the Leongs and the Mallorys all know each other from way back. Anyway David, I've gotta go. Bye."

The last half hour had been such an emotional roller-coaster she felt sick. All she wanted right then was to shut herself up in her own home and bawl her eyes out. It wasn't until much later she was able to let her mind dwell on the amazing coincidence of David living in her old apartment.

Talk about small world, she thought, mulling over the day's events.

Although, really, it goes way beyond coincidence. The only coincidence lies in the apartment being vacant just when he needed a place of his own. This was David automatically returning to a place he'd once referred to as our hideaway from the world.

Her mind reeled.

One way or another, all David's breakthroughs to date had been linked to her. And now this. For a man who'd told her they had no future, and never wanted to see her again, his unconscious mind appeared to be fixated on her.

4

Krista had thought seriously about cancelling her impulsively proposed date, if that was the right term for it. Probably it wasn't, but it was easy to say and a sneaky part of her wished it was.

As expected, Lorna had torn a strip off her for getting in deeper with David. Then she'd surprised her with an unexpected offer of support.

"I suppose you're going to ignore everything I've just said, aren't you Kris?" she'd grumbled. Pulling her friend into an awkward hug, she'd concluded, "Well, if you want to give that grade-A arsehole a second chance, I guess so do I. Bring him round to lunch on Sunday. Dan will be here to take up the slack if the going gets a bit heavy."

With that, she'd hugged Krista again, then urged her out the door with an order to "Go and pretty yourself up. Show him what he's missing."

There were tears in Krista's eyes as she walked round the block to her new house.

She'd always known Lorna was solid gold in the friendship stakes, ever since she'd backed Krista up in facing down the school bully on their first day of high school. The day they first met. Even without knowing as much as Krista, who'd phoned Kate Wilson the night before, ostensibly to see how her husband, Brian, was faring, Lorna had come through with her offer of unconditional support, making Krista's quest to help David her quest as well.

Wiping the moisture from her cheeks, Krista reviewed her conversation with Kate Wilson. After a circuitous discussion covering topics such as how much Kate and the kids missed Brian, and how soon he'd be home again, Krista had led the talk to David Curtis, telling Kate how she was helping him on his memory-hunt. Finally, she slipped in the one question she really hoped for an answer to.

"Did you ever hear anything about an ex-fiancée, Kate? He mentioned her in one of his flash-backs, but I had no idea what to say, since I knew nothing at all about her."

"Her!" Kate's disparaging tone told Krista more than words could have. "I don't like gossiping about David, Krista. He's been through the mill more than any decent man deserves, what with his mother abandoning him, then Sharon, but it's public knowledge, and if it'll help you to help him, …"

Krista made a non-committal sound of encouragement, filing away the reference to David's mother for another time. She listened closely as Kate launched into the story.

"Sharon was one of those high-maintenance, artificial blondes. Placed herself at the centre of the universe and expected everyone else to dance to her tune."

Krista didn't much like the image forming in her mind.

"Not a good fit for a serious career officer like our David," Kate continued. "I wasn't there, but I heard she threw a hissy-fit when he refused to get himself taken off their last deployment. As if it had even been remotely possible! The deployment before this current one, that is, a couple of years back. He was just a lieutenant then, but Brian knew him fairly well since they'd served together before."

Pretty recent history then, Krista thought. *Was he still smarting?*

She grinned to herself as Kate stopped to draw breath and get her thoughts back on track. Ask the right question, and Kate would ramble on until she ran out of steam.

"Anyway, when he got back, she'd shot through with some bloke from Sydney, leaving him with a mountain of unpaid bills. He went after her, but came back alone. He was completely devastated, Krista. Never said what went down, but she's not been seen or heard of in Army circles since, and David has never been the same carefree young man again. It was if she killed something inside him, leaving him hard. Embittered."

Krista nodded slowly, then realised Kate was waiting for an answer.

"Yes. Yes, I think that might fit in with what he said."

And with the way he acted before he went overseas, she added silently, righteously indignant David had tarred her with the same brush as the unknown Sharon.

Couldn't the idiot tell the difference?

"Thanks Kate. I know it goes against the grain for you to spill personal stuff like this. Needless to say, it goes no further."

And it wouldn't. Even Lorna didn't need to know all David's secrets.

Armed with this information, and Lorna's promised support, she'd finally decided to go ahead with tonight's date, vowing to make it her long-term mission to teach David Curtis all women were not like Sharon. Some, herself for example, could be trusted. Maybe nothing would come of it, but nothing ventured, nothing gained; and she'd discovered he still held a huge chunk of her heart to ransom if he only knew it. Which she wouldn't be telling him any time soon.

Arranging her features into a welcoming smile, she got out of her car and went to knock on his door.

David flung the door open, standing triumphantly, supported only by the moonboot encasing his left leg.

"Whoohoo! Look at you! No crutches! That's a major step forward, isn't it, David?"

Genuine joy in his achievement made her carefully manufactured pleasure redundant. This turned the night out into a celebration.

"I thought this day would never come. It felt as if I'd be welded to those bloody crutches for the rest of my life. I'm supposed to use a walking stick, but I reckon it's mostly for show. See, I can get around okay without it."

He tossed it down on the sofa and demonstrated, clomping heavily from lounge room to kitchen and back again.

Krista grinned at his smug pride as he showed off his improved mobility, although, as they later crossed the courtyard to her car, she noted the stick he casually deemed unnecessary was definitely for more than show. He wasn't as steady as he pretended over uneven ground. Still, she was no party-pooper, so she high-fived him and gave him a quick hug before helping him into the Little Yellow Beast, as she'd affectionately dubbed her car.

~~~~~

"Oh. I'm sorry David," Krista apologised on entering *The Boomerang Tavern*. "I wasn't thinking. When we came here that other time, it was on a Friday night. There was a live band, and hordes of people. It was standing room only on the dancefloor. This isn't the same thing at all. It's got none of the atmosphere."

David's gaze followed hers in surveying the quiet, half-empty bar, a bleak look appearing on his face. After yesterday's breakthrough he'd had high hopes their visit would bring a new memory to the surface, only it looked as though there'd be nothing doing. Considering the unknown man he'd privately named Baby's Dad, he couldn't even count a night out with Krista as a plus. Then, glancing at her downcast face, he felt guilty. She'd been generous enough to give up an evening for him. The least he could do was show a bit of appreciation.

"Not to worry, Krissy. Since we're here anyway, we might as well enjoy our meal. We don't have to be working on my bloody memory all the time."

Shortly before their order of steak, salad and thick, chunky wedges with sour cream was delivered, Krista jumped up and headed across the room to the jukebox.

Even though she couldn't magic up the same atmosphere, music had been playing on their first visit, she reasoned, so there should be music playing tonight. Preferably the same songs if she could find them. She programmed as full a playlist as the machine would accept, and headed back to the table.

During the meal they maintained a desultory conversation, mainly on topical issues, steering clear of David's problems by mutual consent. Pushing her plate aside at the end of the meal, Krista noticed David abstractedly tapping his fingers in time with the catchy tune currently playing.

Only one song more to go, she thought, silently debating whether or not to put on a new playlist.

Catching Krista's eye, David commented wistfully, "I'd ask you to dance, but it's way too fast."

Just then the song came to an end and the opening bars of the last song drifted out. An oldie. The slow, romantic *Smoke Gets in Your Eyes* by The Platters. The very song she and David had danced to on the night Krista had hoped to recreate. Did she dare?

I'll be damned if I go tamely home without giving it a go, she answered herself.

Acting before she could talk herself out of it, she jumped to her feet and rounded the table to stand at David's side, striking a theatrical pose.

"Ladies' choice, Captain Curtis. Dance with me? Or are you too chicken?

~~~~~

Stopping off at The Boomerang Tavern before returning home, Krista had been having fun on the night out with her new Army buddies, Kim Lawrence and the other two female soldiers who'd been her companions throughout the week. A group of local men who'd been coming onto them in a good-natured way had pulled their table up alongside, guaranteeing them a selection of no-strings dance partners.

Performing a lively version of the latest dance craze with Jonno, the young builder who'd invited her onto the floor, she looked up to catch a glimpse of a familiar face through the crowd. Casually angling her partner round to give her a clearer view, she confirmed her first impression.

Captain David Curtis was nonchalantly propping up the bar over in the far corner of the room. Watching her? Maybe. It was hard to tell with all the coming and going between them. Her pulse rate quickened from causes other than the energetic dance. After their mutually disapproving beginning, he'd loosened up a bit, and over their shared table at dinner in the Mess each night, they'd discovered quite a bit of common ground. Enough that they were never at a loss for a topic of conversation. She even surprised him into displaying a wickedly dry sense of humour she was sure he didn't reveal to everyone.

By the end of the week she'd actually developed a bit of a crush on the very correct young officer.

Seeing him here, tonight, she felt a pang of regret that she'd probably never see him again. His unit was on overseas deployment next month, and who knew where they'd end up when they returned to Australia at the end of it. She thought their home base was somewhere down south. Enoggera. Or maybe it was Singleton. Not Townsville, that was for sure.

The music stopped, and returning to their table with Jonno, Krista made her farewells.

"Ladies, it's been wonderful getting to know you. Hope all goes well on your deployment. You've all got my email address, so if you want to keep in touch, I'd love to hear from you. David Curtis is over there," she nodded her head towards the bar. "I'll just have a word with him, then I'm heading home."

A few minutes later she sashayed up to David. He knew she was there. He'd watched her cross the floor towards him, making her glad she'd chosen to wear a flattering dress that showed off slim, shapely legs which had been hidden within camouflage trousers all week.

Warm, chocolate-brown eyes assessing her finer attributes, he nodded a silent greeting.

Just then the band came back, playing the introductory bars of an old Platters favourite. Krista leaned close, hamming it up with a Mae West imitation to disguise a sudden attack of nerves.

"Ladies' choice, Captain Curtis. Dance with me? Or are you too chicken?"

A smile that began in his eyes then migrated south to turn up the corners of those deliciously well-shaped lips, answered her without words.

"Chicken? Who are you kidding Mallory? The cream of our country's defenders is afraid of no-one."

Taking her hand, he swung her round in a couple of quick spins which landed them on the dancefloor where he took her in his arms, leading her into a slow waltz which wouldn't have disgraced him on Dancing With the Stars.

"Hidden talents, Captain Curtis?" Krista purred up at him, relaxing and letting him lead her into moves she'd never been game to try before. "You'd have fitted right in with Wellington's army. I've read he required his officers to excel in the ballroom as well as on the battlefield."

"School. Ballroom dancing was compulsory. Meant to civilise us hooligans. I figured if I had to do it, I might as well make a success of it. Impress the girls."

Krista felt sure he'd applied the same if you've got to do it, then do it well philosophy to other areas of his life also. During the week she'd gained the distinct impression he was a man accustomed to success. A driven man who invariably demanded the best of himself.

Finishing with a dazzling series of twirls as the music faded to a halt, Krista was startled to see the other dancers had moved back, giving them the floor to themselves. A standing ovation of whistles and clapping brought a blush to her cheeks.

"Another dance, Krissy?"

David leaned down to make himself heard over the noise, his warm breath feathering across her ear sending ripples down her spine.

Krissy.

No-one else ever called her Krissy. On his lips the pet name sent an exciting shiver rippling down her spine.

"Tempted, David, but no. I want to get home. I only wanted to say thanks for all your help this week. I really appreciated it."

He shrugged, dismissing her thanks.

"I was under orders, but I enjoyed watching you in action, Krissy. If I can't entice you back onto the floor, I might as well call it a night, too. I'll walk you to your car then call a taxi to take me back to the base."

A day or two back he'd begun calling her Krissy, a diminutive no-one else used. The way he said it now, deep and softly sibilant, made it a caress, sending another of those distracting ripples down her spine, awakening the secret places of her body. David Curtis was a dangerous man. He made her think of possibilities she had not considered for way too long a time.

"No need for a taxi, David." Her words had come out sounding too breathless. Too starry-eyed, and that wasn't who she was. She was a mature, sensible woman, not some impressionable teenager. Krista got her breathing under control and finished what she'd begun to say.

"I can give you a lift back to Lavarack. It's hardly out of my way at all."

"Or you could take me home with you."

Did he mean what she thought he meant? Krista shivered, then levelled a steady look at him, taking time to quell the impulse to take him up on his suggestion.

"I'm not that easy, Captain Curtis. It takes more than a twirl on the dance floor to win me over."

He laughed softly, sounding not in the least disappointed, making her wonder whether he'd been testing her in some way. And whether she'd passed or failed. Annoyed, she clicked the doors unlocked and opened the driver's door, waving him round to the passenger side. She didn't like being played with.

They were half-way to Lavarack Barracks before David broke the silence.

"I was out of line, Krissy, but seriously, I would like to see you again. Are you free on Sunday?"

Krista took her time answering, then issued a test for him.

"Not entirely. I've agreed to help out at a birthday barbecue for my twin godchildren Sunday afternoon. They're six, and they've invited a mob of their friends. If you're up to playing lifeguard at the beach, you'll be welcome. I'll cook dinner for you later, if you like. We can watch a movie in, or go somewhere? Whichever you prefer."

It wasn't every man who could cope with a horde of six-year-olds on a sugar high. Krista waited to see if he'd accept the challenge or bale.

"Count me in, Krissy."

He even managed to sound enthusiastic. She smirked to herself, eager to see how he handled the reality. He entered the details she gave him into his phone, then leaned forward to turn the radio up.

"One of my favourite songs," he said, grinning as he began singing along with Ed Sheeran in a surprisingly tuneful baritone.

Arriving at their destination soon after, Krista pulled into the parking area outside the main gate. Expecting David to simply exit and go, she was taken by surprise when, releasing his seatbelt, he leaned over to gather her into his arms. There was nothing tentative about his kiss. It set of a chain reaction of explosions inside her, erasing rational thought. Making her crave more.

When he lifted his lips from hers. Krista pulled his head back down, reclaiming those lips which had been fuelling her fantasies for days.

"I'd better go while I still can. Before we attract the wrong kind of attention," David gasped when he came up for air a second time.

Krista could feel his heart thundering beneath her hand, informing her he was as affected by their kisses as she was. Had it been a mistake not to take him home with her?

"You're a dynamite girl, Krissy Mallory. I'm looking forward to getting to know you better. See you Sunday."

Then he was gone.

A dangerous man, she thought again, the passion-haze clearing from her senses. Now she had regained the capacity for rational thought, Krista knew it was better she took it slowly with David Curtis. She was no one-night-stand. If he wanted a relationship with her, good, but she needed to be sure it was right for her. That he was right for her.

~~~~~

"Dance?" Bewildered, David stared at Krista. "Forgetting something aren't you Krissy?" He tapped his fingers against the moonboot enclosing his gammy leg.

"So you're chicken then? How disappointing. I thought you were up to any challenge. But, if you're not, so be it." She shrugged, anticipating his reaction to her challenge.

"No. I'm not chicken! No way!" He flashed a wicked grin, reminding her more than ever of the man he used to be.

"They're your toes. If you want to risk it, let's go." He got awkwardly to his feet, extending a hand to Krista as she slowly rose from her chair, thinking maybe her challenge was an embarrassing mistake.

She teetered on the brink of reneging. What if he fell? He'd only just been promoted from crutches to walking stick, and here she was demanding he try to dance! She thought regretfully of their amazing waltz from back then. It was highly unlikely he would ever dance with such dazzling proficiency again.

Impatiently tugging on her hand, David clomped ahead of her onto the empty dancefloor.

"Having second thoughts, Krissy? Not allowed! Come on, or the music will finish before we take our first step."

Their shuffling progression round the floor, Krista's arms wrapped tightly around David, holding him upright, fell a long way short of their exhibition waltz. Neither did one huge baby bump inserted between them do anything to add grace to their motion, but it could loosely be termed dancing. If you took into consideration the way their closely entwined upper bodies swayed in time to the music.

Krista was so scared of David falling and further damaging his injured leg, she clung to him, valiantly attempting to keep him upright.

"What was that?" David's startled question coincided with Krista's muffled groan.

"Baby joining in," she muttered. "Did you really feel him kicking his heels up?"

"Yeah. I did. Does that happen often? Getting kicked in the guts like that?"

Krista nodded. "He's quite active. I reckon I've got a footballer in there."

"But … Doesn't it hurt?"

She laughed out loud at the peculiar expression on his face. Men just didn't have a clue, did they?

"It's a bit uncomfortable at times, but it doesn't actually hurt. Unless he catches me under the ribs. Anyway, David. The music's stopped. Let's go."

She carefully moved back from him without leaving him unsupported. She'd carried out her experiment and wasn't prepared to risk any further moves on the dancefloor.

Not that the experiment appeared to have produced results. David's brooding attention seemed entirely focused on the baby as he watched the undulations of its movement disturbing the lie of her dress.

They were in the car on their way home before David revealed the direction his thoughts had taken.

"Your partner, doesn't he mind you spending so much time helping me?"

"Partner?"

Bewildered, Krista stared at him.

"You know. Your baby's father. Doesn't he mind?"

She'd avoided giving him an answer when he'd mentioned her mythical partner on Wednesday.

When he'd kissed her.

Krista was sorely tempted to spin him some yarn to satisfy his curiosity, only how would that work when he regained his memory, as she still firmly believed he would. If David realised she'd been telling him lies he'd never trust a word she said again, and rightly so. There was no help for it, she'd have to stick to the truth, only … definitely not the whole truth.

She didn't believe he was ready for the whole truth. Not yet.

"Touchy subject, David," she warned. "Shortest version. Last year I met a bloke I fell head over heels in love with. Problem was, he was just amusing himself. When I started talking about the future, he got cold feet and dumped me. Left town. Later, when Baby made his presence felt, I wrote, but his reply was unequivocal. He didn't want anything to do with us. Ever."

"God, Krista. The bastard's got responsibilities. He needs to be made to face up to them. There's no way you should have to handle this on your own!"

David's heartfelt indignation on her behalf was all well and good. Here, tonight, she believed he meant every word, but Krista would see what tune he sang when he remembered.

"I'm not on my own. I've got good friends I can count on to be there when I need them. Family too, just a short drive down the coast. You've no need to feel sorry for me, David Curtis."

"Still, …"

"End of discussion." Krista cut in before David could finish his sentence.

"Not your problem, David. You just concentrate on your own concerns. Get that memory back."

"I'm not sure it's going to return. There's been nothing new, and what I did recall wasn't anything important, was it? I've decided to concentrate on planning for life with a completely clean slate. No old baggage dragging me down. Just a future that's mine to make what I can of."

Krista could easily see the appeal. No baggage. No ties. Just a self-made future.

How wonderful it sounded.

"Problem with that, David. Our subconscious operates by its own rules, and we don't know enough to tell what might happen. What if there's a time-bomb in your past? What if it goes off, blasting your idyllic new life to Hell and back?"

The stubborn set of his jaw showed he didn't like what he was hearing.

"What time-bomb, Krista? What do you know you're not telling me?"

Krista shrugged.

Me and my big mouth!

"I only knew you for a few short weeks, David," she temporised, "but I got to know you well enough to realise you were carrying quite a load of baggage from your past. From before I met you. Stuff you never talked about. Like family, past relationships, what was really important to you. The only way you can learn what all that stuff is, is to remember it. I can't help you."

Relieved to be home, she swung the car through the open gates of the Reef Gardens Apartments, cruising to a stop in front of number five.

"Stay put. I'll come round and help you out."

Neither spoke again till David was safely inside his apartment. Krista turned to leave, but before she could take a single step, David shot out his hand and clamped it round her arm, drawing her in close to his chest.

"If my past is as bad as you're inferring, Krista, I don't want to remember it. But I don't need to recall the past to tell the difference between right and wrong. That bastard who got you pregnant mightn't care, but I do. I care, Krissy. I care about you, and your baby. Count me among your friends. Know I'll be there for you, through thick and thin. You're part of my future, Krissy, and I'm damned sure I'm going to be a part of yours."

He stared into her eyes, waiting to see if she had anything to say to his challenging declaration.

She was silent. Stunned. Krista couldn't have said a word if her life depended on it.

Satisfied he'd got his point across, David lowered his lips to hers in another searing kiss.

A kiss that was one hundred percent deliberate. A kiss which was a promise for the future.

Krista felt the heat of it down to her toes curling up in her sensible flat shoes. She couldn't help responding fiercely, even knowing she shouldn't. Until he remembered the whole truth, getting romantically involved with David Curtis was way too dangerous.

To both of them.

She hadn't been kidding when she'd talked of hidden time-bombs.

FORGOTTEN

When they came up for air, she wriggled loose and fled, forced to turn back at the door to tell him of Lorna's invitation.

5

"You were right, Lorna. You warned me getting involved with David was risky. He's a dangerous man. Not physically, of course. He'd never hurt me in that way. I mean emotionally." Krista finished dicing the vegetables for the salad, glanced at her watch and washed her hands. "I better go pick him up. I told him twelve, and it's quarter to."

"Let Dan go."

Lorna yelled for her husband, then sent him off to fetch David.

"Take the kids with you!" she yelled after him, immediately resuming her interrupted conversation with Krista.

"I'd love to say I told you so, but gloating won't help, will it?"

"Not an iota. But you know, Lorna? I'd still make the same decisions again. The old David broke my heart, but he's gone, at least temporarily. I think I might be falling for the new David all over again, Lorna, although I'm not ready to tell him that. Maybe I never will be. I don't know what I would do if he was ever to let me down again."

Lorna snorted, making her opinion abundantly clear.

"You're an idiot, Kris."

"I know."

Head down, a long swathe of blonde hair shielding suddenly moist eyes from her observant friend, Krista began loading a tray to take outside to the barbecue deck, until, tossing her head, emotions steadying, she turned to face Lorna again.

"I've got my fingers crossed that this time he's worth the risk. You know, Lorna, apart from maybe falling in love with him, I really like the man he is now. Much more than I ever did first time around. Back then I rushed into things without taking the time to get to know the man properly. This David seems more sincere. More honest. Open. I just hope he doesn't revert when he remembers all the bad stuff that made him the lousy rat he turned out to be back then."

"Maybe there was no 'bad stuff'," Lorna finger quoted. "Maybe he was just born a bastard. Ever think of that?"

Krista drooped, despondency pummelling at her already weakened defences. But only for a moment.

"Yeah," she agreed, squaring her shoulders and preparing to counter her friend's assertion.

"A few times. More than a few, to be honest, but recently I've learnt a bit about his past I never knew before, and I don't believe he was. I believe he's had a rough life, one way or another, Lorna. I think he has a whole lot of unresolved issues from way before I first met him."

"Well, if you're right, and he does have issues, his psychologist ought to be able to sort him out."

Car doors slammed outside.

"Anyway, Kris, they're back. We can finish talking about this some other time."

Both women turned expectantly towards the door.

"Mum! Mum! Here's Uncle David!"

Jill and Pete, the irrepressible Jansen twins, barrelled through the door, roughly elbowing each other aside as they vied to be first with the news

"He's got a broken leg, so we've gotta be careful not to bump into him."

"He's lost his memory." Jill topped her brother's information. "He doesn't even remember us."

"No! That's unbelievable!" Lorna struck a horrified pose. "How could anyone ever forget you two."

"Muu-um!"

Amid the laughter, David limped into the kitchen, using his walking stick to ensure a safe space around himself rather than leaning on it. Smiling an unspoken greeting at Krista, he turned his attention to his hostess.

"You must be Krista's friend, Lorna. Thanks for inviting me."

Hands on hips, Lorna eyed him from head to toe before slowing reaching to accept his proffered hand.

"You're welcome, David. Dan," her eyes shifted to her husband who'd quietly entered the kitchen behind their guest. "It's getting a bit crowded in here. Why don't you take David and the kids outside and get the barbie flashed up?"

"Come on, Uncle David." Jill took his free hand and carefully led him onto the deck overlooking the pool.

"Can we swim before lunch, Mum? We told Uncle David to bring his swimmers." Jumping impatiently, Pete tugged on his mother's hand.

"If your father's prepared to keep an eye on you." Krista cocked a brow in Dan's direction.

"C'mon Mate. Although I reckon Dave might prefer a beer in the shade."

Cuffing Pete lightly, Dan ushered his son outside, leaving the kitchen once more a spacious, airy workplace. Krista picked up the tray laden with plates, glasses and cutlery and went to set the outdoor table, taking a moment to toss a beachball over the pool fence when Pete called out, asking for 'Someone' to save him having to leave the pool to fetch it.

"I saw what you mean, Kris," Lorna said softly, with a self-conscious glance towards where the men were standing beside the barbecue, when she returned to the kitchen. "I looked him in the eye, and he met my gaze, as if he had nothing to hide. As if he found me worthy of his notice. The old David used to look right through me. Used to really annoy me. A real arrogant bastard, I used to think."

She scooped a mouthful of dip up with a celery stick, crunching it between strong white teeth, grinning at her friend. "Just saying. I'll hold judgement for the time being. See how he shapes up."

"Thanks, Lorna. I'll appreciate not having you on my case every time we talk."

"Oh, well. I'm not promising that! Come on. Let's go join the gang," she added, dodging nimbly when Krista swatted at her with a handtowel.

Outside, Dan was telling David about the new boat he had acquired for his business of ferrying tourists out to the reef on diving and fishing expeditions.

"Business is good, Dave, with all this eco-tourism stuff. Pretty much what we've always done, but now we put a new spin on the advertising. This new addition to our fleet represents a major expansion to *Jansen Reef Tours*. Just telling Dave, here, about the *Chelonia mydas*, Lorn."

He waved his wife to a chair, getting up to fetch a glass of chardonnay for her and a pineapple juice for Krista without being prompted.

"Interested in boats, are you David?" Lorna cocked an eyebrow in his direction.

"Not sure. It's wait and see on that, but I've been reading up on eco-tourism in the region. It feels like something I might like to try when I'm able-bodied again." He gave a self-deprecating shrug. "Always supposing there's room for another operator, that is."

Lorna caught her husband's eye, a silent conversation being exchanged in a blink, then turned to speak to their guest.

"Come and talk to us when you're ready, David. We can probably give you a few pointers. I'll email you the links to some useful websites. In the meantime, why not join us next weekend when we put the *Chelonia* through her paces before she joins the tour fleet."

"Hey Uncle David," Pete called from the pool, interrupting the adult conversation. "Do you know what a Chelonia mydas is?"

"No, Mate. Something nautical perhaps?"

"Nooo. It's our favourite animal in all the world," chimed in his sister while Pete hooted at their guest's ignorance.

"It's the green sea turtle," elucidated Pete, eager to share his knowledge. "We might see one next weekend when we take the new boat out."

"Then I'd better come along. That's if you're sure?" David turned to the adult Jansens for confirmation.

"Wouldn't have asked if we weren't." Lorna laughed as she and her husband spoke in unison.

Watching, Krista couldn't help envying her friend the close personal and working relationship Lorna had with Dan, a man she had no hesitation classifying as a prince among husbands. For a moment she felt sorry for herself.

No loyal, loving husband for her.

No proud daddy for her baby. If only …

Shaking her head, she silently berated herself for giving in to negative thoughts. She was entirely capable of giving her child a good life on her own. More than capable. An established fact, since all her plans for the future were plans for a mother and child alone. Although the right man would be a wonderful addition, a man was not a necessity in her life.

Until David had erupted back onto the scene so unexpectedly, she had come to terms with her lot.

Damn the man! Damn this confusing uncertainty he'd stirred up. And damn the weak, hormone-driven tears stinging her eyes.

Head averted, Krista shot her to her feet abruptly, the bathroom providing an urgently needed refuge. A few minutes later there was a discreet knock on the door.

"You okay in there, Kris?"

"Sure, Lorna." Krista splashed water on her face and reached for a towel to pat it dry. She heard her friend shuffling her feet outside. "No worries," she added. "Baby making a nuisance of himself." Mentally apologising to the baby, she added wryly, *Wonder what excuse I'll be using next month?*.

Ready to face Lorna's concerned scrutiny, she emerged from the bathroom with a cheerful smile tacked firmly in place.

In the kitchen, Lorna was kneeing the fridge shut, both hands holding bowls of food.

"Is it time to fetch the salads? I'll give you a hand."

"Lorn!"

At Dan's shout, Lorna turned pale. Thrusting the bowls into Krista's hands, she raced outside, Krista hard on her heels. A quick survey showed Jill and Pete standing unhurt on the lawn, looking towards the deck, mouths agape. Dan, arms wrapped around David, was glancing over his shoulder with an agonised "What do I do now?" expression on his face which quickly turned to relief when the women appeared on the scene.

"Not sure what just happened," he explained, steering David into the chair Lorna pulled up next to him.

"Pete chucked the ball, yelling at Dave to catch it. Next thing he seemed to lose his balance. Dropped his stick, so I grabbed him before he went over the edge of the deck. Then he went all limp."

"Sorry! Sorry Dan. Think I blacked out for a moment." David closed his eyes, shaking his head slightly. "Okay now. Another memory flash. It caught me by surprise when I was already off-balance, turning too quickly. Thanks for catching me before I hit the deck, Mate."

"So, what've you remembered this time, David?"

Beside the table where she'd dumped the salad bowls, Krista stood stock-still, left hand held to her heart, straining her ears not to miss the answer to Lorna's question.

"As I turned to catch the ball, suddenly I was back in the park along The Strand, catching another ball he threw at me." He turned to look for Krista. "It was Lorna and Dan and the kids with us at the rock pool that day, wasn't it? Some special event? Not sure, but I think I remember birthday balloons and a pack of kids besides Jill and Pete."

"It was our birthday!" Pete raced up, followed closely by his sister.

"We went swimming in the rock pool, then we played in the park and had the party," Jill corroborated.

"It was that red-haired boy who tossed the frisbee into the tree, wasn't it?" David asked excitedly. "I remember now. It was a really fun day."

6

"The kids' birthday was a fun day, and I suppose it's good to remember a bit more, but it's not enough, Krista! I'm only recalling little snippets. Nothing important." Frustrated, David thumped the padded arm of the lounge chair. Back in his apartment with Krista, the Jansen's barbecue long over, they'd been discussing his latest memory flash.

"Who am I, really? What kind of man was I, Krissy? That's what I need to remember, not playing catch with a mob of kids. Today I got the feeling Lorna and Dan were in two minds about me at first. Like you were. Somehow, I'm not liking myself much if decent people have such reservations about the bloke I was back then."

He looked so down Krista longed to throw her arms around David and assure him he was a wonderful man, that he was mistaken; only it wouldn't be true. Not about then. And he was astute enough to call her on it if she attempted to prevaricate.

Love, or maybe it was merely lust, had dazzled her when she'd begun going out with him last year, which was why she'd been so badly hurt when her bubble burst.

Naively, she'd believed they were on the same page, their story about to be completed with love, marriage and happy ever after.

Right up till she discovered they weren't.

With David's plane leaving in the morning, there had been no time to get to the bottom of his hang-ups regarding love and marriage.

Caught flat-footed, she'd been left floundering, her heart in tatters as she watching his plane disappear into the west.

He'd left her no option other than accepting his repudiation of her love for him, however much it hurt. Which it did. A lot. The one time she'd reached out to him since, his terse answering letter, reiterating his parting words, had utterly destroyed her lingering hopes.

Now he was back.

The same in so many ways, but maybe not in the most important one to her if she dared to trust fate. Now he was reaching out to her instead of pushing her away.

Had more than one seed had been left in the wasteland of broken dreams? Hope was sending out new shoots she was almost too afraid to nurture.

David turned to her now, seeking friendship. Maybe love, if his kisses spoke truthfully, although surely he couldn't have fallen in love so rapidly. But how would he react when he remembered everything?

She didn't dare lie. Truth, however painful, was all she had to offer him until she knew what kind of man David was now.

But … Not the whole truth all at once. She lay a protective hand over her baby-bump.

"You made mistakes, David." Krista tempered the bitter truth. "I told you there were issues you hadn't come to terms with. From before I knew you. It's my belief they're the reason you behaved badly, setting my friends and I against you. Hard as it is, we want you to remember those issues so you can address them properly. Please understand, we all support you in your memory quest and want to help you in the best way we can."

She reached out, covering his clenched fist with her hand. Rewarded when he opened his fingers, turning them to clasp hers. However, if anything, his expression became even bleaker.

"What if I never remember, Krissy?"

Krista drew in a lungful of air, considering her next words carefully.

"Then you make this your second chance. Decide who you want to be, and *be* that man. Decide what beliefs are important to you, and *live* by those beliefs." Krista's voice shook with the passion of her words.

"David, not everyone is fortunate enough to be able to remake themselves as the person they most want to be. You can. Then, if you do remember, look at the past through the eyes of the man you are today. The man you truly believe you are meant to be."

Rising from her chair, she rubbed her back. She'd missed her afternoon rest, and a nagging backache was the result. Allied with the stress of their conversation, she'd reached her limit.

"I've got to get going, David. I'll call you in a day or so and we can go somewhere. Another picnic maybe. You were never much into fancy restaurants and hotels, and the picnic outings seem to be paying dividends, even if they only revive seemingly trivial memories for now. Those small recollections all indicate your memory *is* returning. Please. Don't give up hope."

David rose to his feet beside her. Wrapping his arms around her, he rested his forehead on her shoulder.

"My mind doesn't remember us, Krissy, but my body does. I feel certain we were a lot more than simply friends. The way I respond to you now, after so short a time, convinces me I loved you back then. I must have, for love to grow so quickly now. And I do love you, Krissy."

As he spoke, he lifted his head, meshing his eyes with hers, holding nothing back in his determination to convince her he spoke the truth. In his eyes Krista read a message of love overshadowed with the pain of loss.

"Only, whatever I did back then, I really hurt you, didn't I? The not knowing about us is driving me crazy. I don't understand how I could have hurt you, Krissy. So badly I sent you rebounding straight into the arms of the bastard who walked out on you and Baby. I'm so sorry Krissy, love. You said I should be the man I want to be, so I will. That man is going to make it up to you both. I promise."

David made his vow with one protective hand resting on her baby-belly.

"I promise, Krissy. I won't let you down again, even if a time-bomb from the past does explode in my face."

Sealing his vow, his lips met hers in a kiss so sweetly solemn Krista felt a tear trickle down her cheek as she kissed him back. She longed to answer his vow in kind, but inner caution and her memories of devastating pain held the words back.

She kissed him again, patted his cheek, and let herself out the door.

~~~~~

Meeting her publisher's deadlines became a race against time for Krista, with the birth of her baby drawing very close. So it was with a tremendous sigh of relief she hit the 'send' button on the last lot of edits late Wednesday afternoon. The morning before had seen her type 'The End' at the bottom of the first draft of her next novel. Rough as it was, the story was written, and she'd be able to work on improving it in snatched moments in between tending to Baby. With those two huge tasks out of the way, she could concentrate on preparing herself to welcome her child into the world with no unfinished business hanging over her head.

With two weeks still to go, she'd give David a little more of her time for his memory quest. They'd talked briefly on the phone each morning, but, unsure of how she felt about his surprising declaration of love, she'd used the irrefutable excuse of deadlines to avoid seeing him. Sunday night he'd left her speechless, using the words she'd longed to hear from him in the past.

Words he'd never uttered then, and categorically refuted when she did.

How she longed to believe in David. To trust him.

How she feared trusting his love. Trusting him not to break her heart all over again.

I have to think for both of us now.

Rubbing her belly where she felt Baby stretching and changing position, she settled in to do just that. Waiting for the kettle to boil for a cup of peppermint tea, Krista mentally weighed two opposing possibilities.

Maybe love would work out for them this time around. She, David and Baby might find happiness together. Build a good life together.

Or … Once again, it could all come to nothing, if David's time-bomb blew up and he reverted to his previous self – Lorna's Grade A arsehole. She winced, but the coarse, ugly term matched his past actions.

If he did, she'd be left exactly where she had been before he'd reappeared in her life. On her own. Although, with Baby, she'd never be truly alone again.

Making a snap decision to trust in fate and reach for the stars, Krista picked up her phone.

"David. Congratulate me," she began with a laugh. "I've cleared my desk. No more work for a few weeks. Are you free to celebrate with me?"

~~~~~

Although the food at one of Townsville's best restaurants was superb, it was a fairly tame celebration, what with the guest of honour being restricted to mineral water and her date keeping her company.

However, the excitement fizzing through Krista's veins every time she met David's eyes across the table more than made up for the lack of any alcoholic buzz. She spoke no words of love, but her heart spoke for her through her sparkling eyes and her smiling lips.

"Here's to the new book, Krissy." David lifted his glass in a toast, and Krista giggled as she clinked hers against it.

Just then the waiter came to clear away their plates, asking if they wanted to see the dessert menu.

"Krissy?"

"No." She smiled apologetically at the waiter. "That was a beautiful meal, but I've had enough, thank you."

A fleeting frown crossing his brow, David glanced at her less than half-empty plate.

"Are you sure you've had enough? You've eaten barely anything."

"I've sampled everything, and it was all absolutely delicious, but you know, David, I find I do better with very small meals these days. Not much space left inside me the way Baby's growing." She laughed again and patted her bulging tummy.

"How much longer? You look awfully big to me."

"Weeks to go yet." Tossing her hair, Krista airily brushed David's query aside, leaning across the table to pat his hand. Using the plural was still legitimate. Just. "Relax. I'm not going to suddenly land you in the middle of a medical emergency. I would like to go home now though. These very elegant chairs aren't particularly kind to pregnant ladies. How about we go back to my place for coffee?"

~~~~~

Krista sighed, and stretched luxuriantly, flexing her bare toes. It was such a relief to be able to kick off her shoes and put her feet up on her own supremely comfortable sofa while David made her a refreshing cup of tea. If she leaned her head right back she could see him coaxing a coffee for himself out of her state-of-the-art machine in the corner of the kitchen. It hadn't seen much use recently, but he'd assured her he could operate it, and she'd taken him at his word.

"Right. Here you are. One peppermint tea for the mother-to-be, and a cappuccino for me." David returned to the lounge room bearing two steaming mugs. Handing one to Krista, he put the other aside, lifting her feet onto his lap as he sat at the other end of the sofa.

"Ummm. That feels good," she murmured. "Clever of you to guess a foot massage is exactly what I need right now." Cradling her mug in both hands, she lay back, surrendering to David's ministrations. "You've got magic in those hands, David," she purred. "They didn't teach you that in the Army."

"They didn't. The Army doesn't care about pregnant ladies and their tired, aching feet. I've been doing some reading on ways I can help you, Krista my darling, and the writer of one of the articles I found waxed lyrical about the beneficial pleasures of foot massages. Last week I had my physio show me how to do it. Only you're so independent I thought I'd never get the chance to try out my newly acquired skills."

"I might have to book you to make a home visit every evening, Dr Curtis. Aaah …" David dug his thumbs into the tight knot of muscle, releasing pent-up tension.

"Anytime, Darling. It would be my pleasure."

"And mine."

Definitely mine, Krista thought, lying limp and relaxed as his hands became subtly caressing in their application. When those oh-so-wonderful hands eased their way above her knees, though, she regretfully decided it was time to call a halt. The foot massage was becoming too much of a good thing, arousing needs and wants she'd successfully subjugated for months. Needs and wants she was in no condition to satisfy in the manner she'd most like.

She wanted David.

Wanted him with her whole heart, mind and body. Especially body, but her conscience held her back.

Right now, she'd be guilty of taking advantage of him if she accepted the love he was offering, unaware of what had happened between them. She'd be forever guilty of measuring him against past mistakes. Forever waiting for him to backslide.

Best to wait. If he hasn't remembered in a reasonable time, I'll have to tell him. And hope this time love outweighs ingrained prejudices. I'll wait till after Baby is born.

"Gosh, Krissy, I must be good at this. You're almost asleep."

Thinking about how much she loved David, Krista hadn't realised her eyelids had closed, until, at his comment, they fluttered open again. A yawn she couldn't hold back was quickly covered behind her hands.

"For a soldier, you make a wonderful masseur," she teased, smiling sleepily, "and I must be tireder than I realised."

"I'll go and let you get off to bed, Krissy darling. Don't come out," he added, waving her back when she swung her legs to the floor. "It's only a short walk, and I need the exercise."

Ignoring his strictures, Krista swung her feet to the floor add padded towards the door in his wake.

Half-way there, he turned back. A worried frown creasing his brow, he blurted out the question which had been bothering him for some time. He wasn't sure it was any business of his, but Krista was his woman and he couldn't hold back any longer. Wouldn't.

"Krissy, what if the baby comes early? Maybe you shouldn't be here on your own. I could stay if you like. Just so you're not alone. No strings."

"Oh David, that's so sweet of you." Krista rose awkwardly to her feet and crossed the room to lean against him, reaching up to pat his cheek. "It's not necessary though. Lorna is just round the block and can be here in five minutes if I call. I won't be on my own much longer, anyway. Mum is arriving next week and will stay on for a while after I bring Baby home."

Sliding both arms around his neck, she did what she'd been wanting to do for ages. Putting her heart and soul into the kiss, she told him in actions what she wasn't ready to tell him with words.

"Goodnight, David. See you Sunday."

Gently, she eased him the rest of the way to the door, opening it to wave him on his way.

7

Once out of the harbour, the *Chelonia mydas* skimmed across the glinting, mirror-smooth waters of the Great Barrier Reef with the ease of her namesake. Glistening herself from a liberal application of sunscreen, Krista lay back in one of the comfortable chairs provided for the paying passengers, none of whom were present today, this being strictly a family outing. The breeze ruffling her hair, she idly watched Dan instructing David in steering the boat. Her skin tingled anew as she relived the precious moments David had spent rubbing sunscreen onto her back before they set sail.

Unconsciously, his hands had fallen into the same gently arousing rhythmic strokes her body recognised them using on another day as perfect as this one when it was just the two of them enjoying a day out on the water in a hired motor-cruiser.

~~~~~

"Don't fuss, Krissy. I'm fine. Look how tanned I am," David had protested when Krista insisted he use sunscreen.

"And what about when you take your shirt off? Go on, show me." Laughing, Krista had tugged his shirt up over his head as she spoke. "See! Not so tanned there. Stand still." She'd slathered the lotion generously over his back and chest, her hands gradually slowing to gentle caressing strokes, grinning to herself when she noticed the flow-on effect her actions were having on certain parts of his anatomy.

"Your turn."

Impatiently, David pushed her unbuttoned beach jacket down her arms letting it puddle on the tiny deck around her feet, leaving her standing there clad only in her brand new, very skimpy sunshine-yellow bikini. Filching the tube of sunscreen from her fingers, he set about returning her favour. With interest. Drawing out the provocative application of creamy lotion till her legs quivered with the effort of standing still under his skilful hands.

Krista knew she'd never use sunscreen again without remembering, and yearning to repeat, this moment.

Time to turn the tables.

Rising up on her toes, Krista slid her body over David's slick torso. Linking her arms behind his head, she gave in to her burning desire, and kissed him. Long and deep. A kiss he met with matching enthusiasm, his large hands cupping her derriere and hauling her tight against his rampant masculine attributes.

"Hey, you two! Get a room!"

The young hoon at the wheel of the boat next to them gunned his engine, his flaring bow-wave rocking their boat in his wake, his passengers roaring with laughter.

One arm supporting Krista on the unsteady deck, David gave their tormentors the finger as they sped off far quicker than marina regulations permitted.

"Sorry, Krissy." David landed a last brief kiss on Krista's lips and stepped away. "We'd better get going. This is no place for where we were heading just now."

Blushing a fiery scarlet, Krista, as the one with the boating licence, slid into the skipper's chair while David cast off. Moving more sedately than the boat rapidly disappearing ahead of them, they puttered out of the marina following the channel markers out into Cleveland Bay and on to the open sea where they increased speed, setting course for a lesser-known section of reef where there was good snorkelling.

~~~~~

"Dolphins! Look everyone! Dolphins!"

Pete's shout snapped Krista back to the present.

There were dolphins that day, too, she mused, clinging just a moment longer to her pleasant reverie. She'd always loved the beautiful, graceful animals and it had warmed her heart to see David, her big, tough soldier, utterly entranced by their antics as they'd surfed the bow-wave of the speeding boat.

She got slowly to her feet, clutching at the back of her chair as the *Chelonia* dipped into a small trough then righted itself again. Carefully mindful of her precious cargo, she made her way to the rail to lean against David's shoulder. His arm wrapping round her expansive waist, drawing her into his side, seemed an automatic gesture.

Krista didn't know whether or not their easy familiarity with each other was entirely a good thing.

Depends on the eventual outcome, I suppose, she mused, snuggling closer. An anticipated outcome with which she was daily feeling more comfortable. A private little smile curved her lips as she shook her hair back and lifted her face to the warm breeze caressing her skin.

The dolphins stayed with them for almost ten minutes, leaping, diving and tail-walking with an enthusiasm utterly delighting their human audience, until, with no discernible signal, the pod turned as one and sped off at a tangent. Playtime over, and back to the serious business of survival? Krista wondered, straightening with a contented sigh to step away from the rail.

Shortly after, Dan throttled back the powerful motors letting the Chelonia coast to a stop in shallow water close to the edge of the reef. The anchor, settling to the clear, sandy bottom, held her in place, bobbing gently on the low swell. Facemasks, snorkels and flippers were hauled from the storage lockers, and, amid exhortations to

"Stay close to your Mum.";

"Be careful not to touch the coral.";

and

"Don't stray too far from the boat.";

the Jansens took to the water in record time.

Each with a twin in close attendance, Dan and Lorna led the way. Discarding his moonboot, David slung the new Nikon underwater camera he'd treated himself to round his neck.

About to follow the others into the water he turned to where Krista sat, pulling on her flippers.

"Maybe you ought to stay onboard, Krissy." Warily eyeing Krista as he spoke, he was taken aback when she laughed at his tentative suggestion.

"Not to worry, darling." Patting his cheek, she helped herself to a long, lingering kiss.

While appreciative of his concern, she had no intention of meekly allowing him to dictate to her, now or ever, and lowered herself carefully into the water. Realising the futility of further remonstration, yet as determined not to let her out of his sight as Dan and Lorna were with their independent pair of waterbabies, David hastily splashed in at her side. Smiling at what she correctly read as genuine worry creasing his forehead, Krista relented.

"My doctor's okay with me swimming, you know." She reassured him. "I checked. And actually, David, I feel so much lighter and more comfortable in the water. I promise I'll be sensible."

With another wide, happy smile, she blew him a kiss, popped her mouthpiece in, adjusted her face mask, and, leaving David scrambling to keep up, paddled off in the wake of her friends. Later, when she tired sooner than the rest of their party, he escorted her back to the boat and saw her safely on board before rejoining the others.

Demonstrating his love for her in such a practical, caring way warmed Krista's heart, convincing her, if she needed further convincing, that the decision she was leaning towards was the right one.

Still, there remained that tiny, niggling doubt about how he'd react when he learned the truth.

Better to wait, she reassured herself. *It won't be long now.*

Finally Dan reckoned the twins had had enough and ordered everyone out of the water.

"Aw, Dad. Do we have to?"

Predictably, it was Pete who complained the loudest, but Dan was adamant.

"Sorry Son, but if I don't get my lunch soon, I reckon my stomach just might eat me instead. Besides, I happen to know your Mum's special cheesecake is on the menu."

The promise of his favourite dessert clinched the deal and Pete splashed madly off to catch up with his sister who was eagerly regaling Krista with an account of everything she'd seen.

"... and we saw a turtle," she concluded excitedly. "I didn't think we would, you know Auntie Kris, but just before Dad signalled us to come back, we saw one! It was only a baby, about this big." Jill held her hands about forty centimetres apart, her eyes glowing.

"It was bigger than that," Pete chimed in, elbowing his sister aside. "You know Auntie Kris, it was really good luck, wasn't it, seeing a green turtle on the *Chelonia mydas's* first reef trip?" Barely slowing long enough to take a breath, he rattled on, turning his attention to David who was drying off nearby.

"Did you get a picture of it Uncle David?"

"Sure did Pete. I filmed it swimming past you then disappearing up that canyon between the coral outcrops."

"If you hurry up and get settled, I'll show David how to play his films back on the screen. He might even let me make a copy of it for you, like Sylvia does for the tourists."

Lorna explained to David, "Sylvia's a freelance photographer who's agree to come on the *Chelonia* with Dan and his deckhand, Myra. She films the day, then on the way home edits it down to a thirty minute video which everyone gets as a courtesy souvenir that's built into the cost of the tour. Quite a few go on her website and order other photos and printed memorabilia as well. I believe she does rather well out of it, and it's a little extra our clients get that not everyone else offers. If you're serious about joining the tourist trade, it's something to consider, David. People like a 'free'," she finger quoted, "souvenir to take away with them."

Her friend's willingness to share professional tips gave Krista another warm glow. Lorna was a friend in a million. While not shy about voicing her opinion in no uncertain manner, her allegiance, once granted, could be relied on to Hell and back.

"Don't go mucking about with films now, Lorn," Dan chipped in impatiently. "It's time to head over to the island and get lunch organised." As he spoke, he hauled up the anchor and got underway, steering the boat towards a tiny tropical islet a short distance away. Nosing in as close as he could, he anchored again in water shallow enough for them to wade ashore carrying the cooler bags containing the picnic Lorna and Krista had packed that morning.

Lunch over, the twins clamoured to go exploring.

"Off you go, too," Krista urged, making shooing motions at Lorna and Dan.

"You know you'd both rather go exploring with your kids than pack this lot up. I can manage. Then Baby and I will have a little rest here in the shade."

"I'll help." David added his voice to Krista's.

"C'mon Mum. I need you to help me find shells." Jill tugged at her mother's hand.

"Well, as long as you're sure."

Hugging her daughter, Lorna smiled and winked at Krista and David. Hand in hand with Jill, she ran a few metres up the beach to catch up with Dan and Pete who'd already set off.

"Sure you don't want to go exploring too?" Krista raised an eyebrow in David's direction.

"Nah. They don't need me tagging along, and anyway, I'd rather spend the time with you, Krissy. Besides, I don't want to overdo it. This is the longest I've been on my feet without the boot."

"I wondered about that. You seem to be moving more easily every time I see you."

"I am. The physio reckons it won't be long till I can ditch it altogether. It feels like the leg's been out of action forever, so it's really important I be careful a bit longer, no matter how impatient I get. The last thing I want is a setback at this stage."

They'd been efficiently repacking the picnic debris while they talked, and now David shook out the rug and spread it in the shade. Settling onto one corner with his back against a convenient boulder, he patted the space beside him.

"Lie down here, Krissy darling, and use my lap as a pillow."

A rosy blush stained her cheeks as Krista obediently made herself comfortable with her head resting against David's thigh.

What's wrong with me? She grumbled silently to herself, annoyed by her self-consciousness. *I've done a whole lot more with him than use him as a pillow.*

All the same, she felt a deep sense of intimacy lying with David on the glistening white coral sand beach, rich turquoise water lapping quietly at the low-tide line and the fading calls of children's voices mingling with those of a distant flock of terns. Especially when David wrapped his arms around her, leaning down to press a gentle kiss onto her forehead.

Without conscious thought, Krista reached up her hand, laying it against David's cheek. At the same time tilting her head towards him. Needing no further invitation, David's next kiss was upon her lips. A kiss in which Krista willingly met him more than half-way. His hands lightly kneaded her fuller than usual breasts, arousing her to purring appreciation.

During the bleak, lonely months following David's defection, she'd almost forgotten the heady pleasure of a man's hands lovingly caressing her body. Their embrace became more heated, until the sound of children's laughter impinged on their awareness. Raising his head, David glanced quickly up and down the beach.

"It's okay," he murmured. "There's no-one in sight, but I guess this is neither the time nor place."

"No, it's not," Krista agreed, making no effort to disguise her regret. She could remember another lonely beach where both the time and place were absolutely perfect for two lovers to indulge their passions.

Reluctantly, she sat up and tidied herself.

Tuning in once again to David, she sat up straighter as he uttered the words she'd have loved to hear back when. She loved hearing them now, even though she was afraid to let herself believe it could be as easy as he made it sound.

"I do love you, Krissy darling," he began. Continuing, he added, "You know, the more time I spend around the twins, the more I realise how much I want children of my own. To be a family man. I meant what I said about loving you Krissy. One day I hope you'll marry me and let me be a dad to your baby." He rubbed his hand over her baby bulge, pausing with a look of wonder on his face as the baby kicked as if responding to his ministrations.

Maybe it is, Krista thought, fervently praying he wouldn't revert back to the old David when his memory returned. She liked …, no, she'd be honest with herself. She loved this new, improved version so very much.

Pulling up the bottom of her shirt, David bent to plant a kiss on her belly.

"I do understand your reasons for not giving me an answer yet, Krissy," he said with a wry smile, "but the uncertainty is killing me."

Sure in her own mind of what she hoped for in the future, Krista encouraged him with her response.

"I don't think you need worry too much what my answer will be, David darling, since I love you too. I just hope you won't change your mind when you remember what made you the man you used to be."

"I'm only hesitating because I want you to be completely certain that marrying me is really what you want," she said, throwing caution to the winds.

"Maybe you could ask your therapist - Dr Zelinka, isn't it? - if it's possible to use something like hypnosis to unlock those dark memories from your past. They're what drove us apart before. I'm sure of it. Then you can lay them to rest and move on."

And I am sure that's the truth, she thought.

The impatient part of her wanted to force him to remember, while the cautious part argued that the longer it took before he had to face his past, the more chance there'd be of his love for her growing strong enough to withstand those dark forces she feared.

Whatever they were.

"My next appointment with Dr Zelinka is on Thursday."

David frowned. He could see Krista's point. God knew, he was impatient enough himself to get his memories back, but the thought of hypnosis gave him the cold shivers. Grimly, he stared off into the distance.

"I'll talk to him. I can't go on not knowing if my lack of memory is going to loom over us, threatening our happiness."

Krista leant against his shoulder, putting an arm around him.

"Whatever it takes, Darling, I'll be here supporting you."

Since discussions about David's amnesia invariably made them both feel miserable with their inability to alter his condition, by tacit agreement they changed the subject.

Sitting comfortably in the shade of the beach almond tree, they chatted idly till the Jansen family returned and it was time to leave.

~~~~~

Thinking about his future plans for carving a niche for himself in the tourist trade, David had booked a place for himself on a 4WD tour of the Townsville hinterland on Sunday.

"If I go now while I'm still partially handicapped by this," he tapped the awkward, bulky boot on his left leg while explaining to Krista, "then I'll be able to gauge the provisions I'll need to make for less agile paying clients. Although, mind you Krissy, I'm really hoping to attract the serious adventurers."

"Why not start small doing what you like best, then maybe you can expand into other areas?" Krista replied. "That's the way Dan and Lorna did it. One boat to start with, building up eventually to a whole fleet. The *Chelonia* is their fourth, you know."

So, left to herself on Sunday, Krista prepared for her mother's arrival later in the week, a task all too quickly accomplished. Even spending several hours at her computer, working on her next book, she still had too much time on her hands. Time she spent prowling restlessly from one make-work task to another going over and over in her mind all the arguments she'd had with herself about whether or not she should commit to a future with David.

Arguments about whether or not the return of his memory would affect his present attitude to marriage and a family of his own.

An attitude diametrically opposed to his previous one.

Useless arguments, since her heart was already committed.

Having witnessed his frustration over his amnesia, she felt guilty for withholding what little she knew, only it was such a delicate subject. It would be all to easy to skew anything she said to the way she wanted him to feel, and that felt awfully close to lying.

No. Krista shook her head. *Better for both of us if he remembers for himself. Then we'll talk it over rationally. Hopefully he won't forget what he's feeling now.*

The result was, that by the time David returned from his tour and rang to tell her about it, she was even more impatient for the restoration of his memory than he was.

"Sounds as if you had a good day, Darling, and picked up some very useful tips on conducting organised tours. I guess it must be a lot like conducting training exercises in the Army in some ways."

David agreed, but Krista barely listened, her mind still distracted by thoughts of their problematic future.

"Are you free on Tuesday," she blurted out, interrupting him. "It's just that there's one more place, Hidden Cove, I'd like to take you to. We'd have gone there ages ago except your leg wasn't up to it since there's a fairly steep set of steps cut into the cliff to get down to the beach. There's a handrail and a couple of zig-zags, so I reckon you can manage it okay now."

"I guess." David sounded less than eager. "What about you, though, Krissy? You're not exactly at your most agile. Maybe we ought to put it off."

No way! If anything can break though his brain-fog, Hidden Cove should.

But she held her tongue. No way could she put that sort of pressure on him.

"No problem, Darling. I'm still quite fit, but I promise to take it slowly and carefully. Hidden Cove is a really special little beach and it used to be one of your favourites. Let's have one last picnic together before I put my feet up and wait for Baby." She tried to make her voice a bit off-hand, downplaying the importance she placed on the visit, Hidden Cove being the last place she could think of which might jog something loose in David's elusive memory.

8

Tuesday was another gloriously sunny day with the promise of showers in the late afternoon. Nothing to deter Krista from her planned day at Hidden Cove. Glad both she and David preferred the Great outdoors to more urban pursuits, she hummed to herself as she packed yet another picnic for two. Excitement fizzed through her veins at the thought of the memories the day might unlock.

How wonderful if David remembers for himself before Baby arrives. Time's running very short for that to happen.

Wonderful indeed, and it would save her from having to tell him things she knew he wouldn't be happy to hear. If it came to that, she'd have to hope he didn't shoot the messenger. Or the equivalent, and turn his back on what they were discovering together.

The doorbell rang, putting an abrupt end to her musings. Annoyed at the interruption, she flung the door open, determined to send her importunate caller on their way quick-smart so she could get round to pick David up at the appointed time.

"David!" Krista gaped at him. "I was about to go over to your place. There was no need for you to walk round."

A smug grin curving his mouth up at the corners, David leaned forward, kissing her hungrily on her open mouth. Then again, taking his time about it until Krista's toes curled into the carpet and she felt a tingling ache low in her pelvic region.

"Umm. More," she demanded when he lifted his mouth from hers. A wolf-whistle from a tradie on his way to work finally reminded them they were standing in an open doorway. Krista giggled, tugging at David's hand to draw him inside so she could shut the door.

"Not yet, Darling," he smirked. "I've got something to show you first."

David stepped aside, flinging his arm wide.

"Look! I didn't have to walk round, Darling. I drove. What do you think?"

Leaning on his shoulder, Krista stepped curiously onto the doorstep beside him, taking in the sight of a brand-new charcoal grey Toyota Troopcarrier parked at the kerb. Her breath hissed as she inhaled sharply.

"David! What have you been up to?" Krista choked back a sudden burst of laughter. "Well, obviously, you've got yourself a pretty impressive set of wheels. When? Why didn't you tell me. This is exciting, Darling. Is it for your business? You don't need something that big for around town."

She waddled quickly past him and circled the vehicle, opening the door to peek inside.

"This thing's a monster!"

"I ordered it a couple of weeks back when I decided on what I want to do. It needs to be fitted out for passengers, and I'll get it painted up with my company name and a rainforest picture of some sort. Lorna recommended an outfit which does that sort of work. She's also offered to walk me through all the paperwork involved in setting myself up as a tourist operator."

"I hadn't realised you were that far advanced in your planning." How had all this been going on under her nose and she hadn't had a clue?

David had the grace to look a trifle sheepish.

"It kept me busy while I wait for you to make up your mind about us," he teased, ducking her playful swat.

"Seriously though, David. You don't think you're rushing things a bit?"

"Nope. I know what I want and couldn't see the point in letting the grass grow under my feet. I hope to be ready for business in another two or three months. By then I'll be fit enough to take small groups out on adventure hikes, sightseeing, etc."

"Well, I'm impressed. You seem to have achieved an awful lot in a short time."

"Falling in love with you has been terrific motivation, Krissy. I'm determined to have more to offer you and Baby than a broken down ex-soldier. Anyway, let's grab your gear and try The Beast out."

"Okay. I notice you've got the boot off again."

What happened to being carful?

David's careless shrug annoyed Krista into speaking more sharply than she felt she was entitled to. His quick frowning glance in her direction implied he thought so too.

"It's a good road so probably it won't put too much strain on your leg, although I can't vouch for the cliff path."

She was the one stalling on making a commitment so she had no right to be put out when David went his own way without consulting her.

Opening her mouth again she modified her tone, bringing back the cheeky smirk which was beginning to grow on her, so she smiled as well.

"Although, since you've already been driving The Beast, I guess it's not bothering you too much."

"No, it isn't. It's an automatic, so my left leg isn't needed, but the boot will be back on for climbing down to the beach. I've no intention of blowing it this close to being back to full use of my bum leg."

"Good. Give me a minute to grab my bags."

Like a perfect gentleman, David went with her to carry her things. Giving her a boost up into the high cab, he took less than gentlemanly advantage of the opportunity to give her rear end a speculative caress.

The drive to Hidden Cove went quickly with David bringing Krista up to date on his business plans. Watching him closely, Krista observed that ploughing full steam ahead into his plans for Curtis Adventure Tours, David appeared to have shaken off the depression which had caused her quite a lot of concern over the previous few weeks.

~~~~~

"Oh good." Krista's eyes sparkled as her gaze surveyed the scene as they pulled off the road into the empty parking lot on what was a busy work day for most people. "Looks like we'll have the beach to ourselves, Darling."

Eager to see what, if any, memories were sparked by this magical spot, Krista hung back, letting David take the lead. The beginning of the path wasn't easy to see until you were right on it, so when he strode unerringly in the right direction without so much as a single glance to either side, she practically danced for joy.

The next test came when they stepped off the path onto the beach at the bottom of the cliff. To the left lay a broad, inviting sweep of golden sand reaching to the foot of the next headland. Most people were happy to claim a spot here, never looking further. Krista held her breath as David turned back to take her hand now they were off the narrow path and able to walk side by side.

Without prompting, he led her off to the right. Towards where a jumble of giant boulders lay scattered over the sand, almost, but not quite, blocking the way to what Krista had always believed to be the true Hidden Cove – a tiny, perfect pocket of beach completely out of sight from the main beach. She'd shown him this private spot the first time she'd brought him here, and they'd made it their own on subsequent visits.

"Since there's nobody about, we may as well put our gear in the cave out of the sun, Krissy. It'll give you somewhere private to change after we swim, too."

Yes! He's remembering this place, all right.

Krista mentally cheered. She'd said not one word about the cave which was still out of sight. Then she bit her lip, telling herself not to get over-confident. He'd automatically recalled other familiar places.

Would he recall why this particular place was so special to her? To them both?

"Good thinking." Casting her doubts aside, she smiled, optimistically sure she'd done the right thing in bringing him here today. Fingers crossed, she padded along at his side.

They had to duck their heads to enter the cave tucked away behind the boulders where the waves had carved it into the base of the cliff, but inside the roof rose high enough for them to walk upright with no danger of hitting their heads. David turned slowly on the spot, studying the dry, sandy-floored space only a little bigger than the average bedroom, a puzzled frown on his face.

Krista hardly dared breath as she watched him.

"It's really private in here, isn't it?" David mused. "If you didn't know it was here, you probably wouldn't bother coming round those rocks with a nice, sandy beach at the foot of the path."

There was a wicked glint in his eyes as he wrapped his arms around Krista, moulding her, baby bulge and all, to him. His forehead resting lightly against hers, voice seductively low, he whispered, "I wonder how many couples have made love in here?" Acting on the thought, he brushed his lips across hers, gradually deepening the kiss.

Krista melted into him, heartbeat accelerating and heat flooding her body.

"Yes! Yes! She silently exalted. *It's working! He's remembering."*

~~~~~

The weather had been iffy enough for David to protest against a day at the beach. Pouting, Krista had protested.

"But it's my favourite beach. C'mon David. So what if it rains. Tropical rain is warm, and we'll get wet swimming anyway. A little water won't hurt us. You're not a cream-puff; you won't melt."

With that insult Krista had prevailed with no further argument from her big, tough fear-nothing soldier.

The sun broke through the billowing cloud mass as they arrived at Hidden Cove to find they were not alone. A scattering of other people occupied the golden crescent of sand at the foot of the cliff path, and David led the way to a spot a short distance to the right, dropping his towel and their picnic cooler approximately half-way between where two other groups had staked their claims.

"Not here, David. Too many people. That spot down there's much better." *She pointed to the far end of the beach where a tumble of giant boulders with the hill rising steeply behind them marked the end of the sand.*

"Shouldn't we stay closer to the path back to the carpark? Just in case that rain comes and we have to make a dash for it? There's no shelter down there."

Ignoring David's cautionary warning, Krista tossed her hair and, grinning to herself, kept walking. Hidden Cove was familiar territory for her. A place she knew very well from childhood explorations during family picnics. But with the tide on the turn, she'd wait till after their swim to share its secrets with David.

"Race you in!" she challenged, dumping her beach-bag on a convenient flat-topped rock. Her sandals and wrap landed in a heap beside it, and laughing, she sped across the warm sand, splashing into the sparkling blue water.

Even with her head-start, David caught her before she was waist deep, grabbing her around the middle and tumbling them both beneath the rippled surface. Coming up spluttering and gasping for air, Krista was again deprived of breath by David's kiss.

Having thrown off his earlier grumpiness, he was at his most playful.

The way Krista liked him best.

Liked, and, dare she admit it? Loved him.

She'd never fallen in love so hard and fast before, but this time was so different to the past. Just as David himself was so different to her previous boyfriends.

He reduced her to helpless, exhilarated, half-fearful longing. This time she felt instinctively she was in for the long haul. Thoughts of white dresses and cooing babies had begun to invade her mind in quiet moments. Neither of them had spoken of love, but in her mind, David Curtis had become 'her man'.

She kissed him back, putting everything she felt for him into her kiss.

"Darling Krissy, you ought to know you can't outrun me. You're my girl, and if you run, I'll catch you. Every time."

A shy blush heating her cheeks, Krista giggled, spinning out of his loose, slippery hold. Swimming a few quick strokes further out into deeper water, she turned back towards him.

"Maybe I like being caught, when it's you doing the catching."

Laughing again, Krista headed straight out to sea at her best, quite impressive, speed, but not for too long. Diving underwater, she reversed direction. Launching a successful surprise attack, she dragged her pursuer under. This time David was the one to surface spluttering and gasping for air to be kissed breathless.

"You see Darling? Two can play at this game."

Krista found herself thoroughly enjoying being the aggressor in their game. Accustomed in his work in the Army to being the leader, David Curtis was such a dominant male she usually found herself relegated to the more passive role. Not that she minded, although cheekily she felt it wouldn't hurt him to play second fiddle every now and then.

On that thought, she kissed him again, wrapping her arms and legs around him so that he was fully supporting her in the water. Through the thin fabrics of their swimmers she felt the hard evidence of his arousal pressing intimately against her and melted into his heat, revelling in her feminine power.

A shiver of excitement rippled through her, and she pressed even closer. Then, easing back a little, she let go, once again slipping from his grasp to lead him on another playful chase.

I really do love this man, she thought again.

She'd never felt this depth of desire before him. Never wanted a man as she wanted him, even though they'd known each other such a short time.

David Curtis was the one for her. The man she wanted to spend the rest of her life with. Every moment they spent together she felt surer of her feelings for him, though they had not yet become lovers, as she'd insisted on getting to know him better before making the decision to enter into such intimacy.

A million things she didn't know about him still remained undiscovered. Things it would take the rest of her life to learn. Even so, she was confident she knew the most important parts of the man.

Some facets of his personality she'd learnt directly, others from observing the respect and liking his men had for him. He was brave, with a strict regard for duty. He was protective of those in his care. He liked children and animals. He was kind, and, although he'd not yet spoken the words, his actions convinced her he loved her.

As she loved him.

While respecting her wish to wait till she was sure of her feelings, he'd never hesitated to let her see his desire for her. A desire she returned in full measure.

So why am I still holding back? *she questioned as she swam cleanly through the water.*

No reason at all, *she answered herself, adding a promise.* Next time. Next time I'll say 'Yes'.

Giddy with anticipation, she threw herself into the flirting game of pursuit and capture she and David were playing.

So wrapped up in each other were they that neither noticed the last of their fellow beachgoers hurriedly departing. Neither did they notice the rapidly approaching storm sweeping in from the sea until a flash of lightning and a deafening thunderclap broke through their self-absorption.

"C'mon Krissy. Out of the water!" David yelled, waiting to see she was headed for the beach before falling in beside her, matching her stroke for stroke. More lightning and a prolonged roll of thunder heralded the rain which began falling in great, heavy drops just as they reclaimed their gear.

"Not that way," Krista called out as David turned to race down the beach to the path up the cliff. "We'll never make it in time. This way. We can shelter in the cave."

At a run she led the way round the boulders into a secluded sandy nook in front of a shallow cave, dashing in as the rain began pelting down in earnest.

"Made it," she called over her shoulder. "Watch your head Darling. It's a bit low for adults."

The cave widened once they were in, the ceiling rising to a comfortable height.

While David gazed around him, Krista spread out her beach mat on the dry, sandy floor and began towelling herself dry. Shortly they were sitting side by side on the mat, staring out at the rain pounding onto the sand.

"It's just a storm," Krista murmured. "It won't last long. We can have lunch while we wait, if you're hungry."

Catching her by surprise, David tumbled her back onto the mat.

Holding her hands above her head, he knelt astride her body, claiming her lips in a deliciously arousing salt flavoured kiss.

"I'm hungry, alright," he murmured, voice harsh with suppressed passion. "Very hungry, darling Krissy, but not for lunch. I'm hungry for you."

He leaned forward again, then, his lips barely brushing hers, he drew back slightly, waiting till her curious gaze was fully locked onto him.

"We've been playing with fire, Krissy, and I'm not sure I can handle much more of it if we continue."

His breath coming in short, hard gasps, he asked aloud the question his eyes had already asked silently.

"Should I stop now, Darling, while I still can, or are you ready to give us both what you know you want as much as I do?"

Reaching her hand up to lay it on his cheek, Krista felt warmed to hear both respect for her wishes and his willingness to share the blame for their arousing waterplay when she knew very well she'd been the one to instigate their teasing games. Maintaining steady eye contact, without hesitation she acted on the decision she'd made earlier.

Next time had arrived.

"Darling David," she said "I'm more than ready."

Blushing at her boldness, she dropped her eyes only to open them wide a moment later. This was David, whom she loved absolutely. There was nothing to feel shy about. Swallowing nervously, she whispered huskily.

"I'm hungry for you, too."

Reaching up both hands Krista locked her arms around his neck, urging him to complete the kiss he'd withdrawn from a few seconds earlier.

To the accompanying rumbling of thunder and the hissing of torrential rain on the sand outside their secure hideaway, they came together in a fury of heat and passion, and speed, helping each other out of their wet, clinging swimwear. Each using hands and mouths to drive the other to the precipice … and beyond. Later, with the noise of the storm receding into the distance, they made love again. Slowly, sweetly and infinitely satisfying.

~~~~~

As Krista revelled in David's kisses and increasingly daring caresses, she relived in memory their loving the first time she'd brought him here to her secret cave in Hidden Cove. They had been so good together, each instinctively knowing just exactly what the other liked. Then, and every time they'd made love in the few short weeks which were all the time they'd had together before David flew out on his overseas posting to the Middle East.

How could he have thrown it all away without warning? Without explanation?

How could she trust he wouldn't do it again?

She couldn't. Which was why she had to wait for his memory to return and see what happened then, however much she wanted to take advantage of this gentler, more vulnerable, David who offered her everything she most wanted.

Reluctantly Krista eased herself out of his embrace.

"Is it time to swim?" he asked, voice low and rasping, steadying her as she moved away.

"That's probably a good idea," she said when she'd regained her power of speech.

"I can't give you what you want, David, and it's not fair to lead you on like this and not deliver."

"No need to apologise, Darling. I understand your reservations, even if I don't necessarily agree with them. Besides," he rubbed a hand over her baby bulge with a speculative downward glance. "You're probably not up for what I've got in mind, even if you did agree. You seem awfully big for someone with a few weeks to go. Are you sure you've got your dates right?"

Guiltily, she followed his gaze.

No question she had her dates right. It just wasn't the vague 'few weeks' time' she'd told him, not wanting to put extra pressure on him. A decision she now regretted in part, but felt she couldn't change at this point.

If only he'd *remember!*

She'd had such high hopes of this visit to Hidden Cove, and it had started out so promisingly. Now he seemed to have lost that spark of contact with the past and be firmly entrenched in the present again.

"Off you go while I change. I'll meet you down by the water."

This time there were no seductive games of chase and catch. David hovered protectively close, setting Krista's nerves on edge with his solicitous hovering. Until she told him she wanted to rest in the shade.

"You go off and have a decent swim," she urged when he offered to keep her company. "Give that leg a good workout."

It hadn't taken too much coaxing to persuade him to take some time out for himself.

Later, with Krista's usual good humour restored by her period of quiet reflection in the shade, they enjoyed a leisurely picnic lunch then slowly made their way back up the cliff to the carpark. By the time they reached the top, Krista was puffing heavily, her hands bracing her back while Baby kicked madly making her groan.

"You look as if you've overdone it."

David's critical comment raised Krista's hackles all over again. Especially as it was entirely justified. Biting her tongue, she grudgingly conceded the point.

"Maybe a bit. That path is steeper than I've been used to lately. Just give me a minute to get my breath back." She reached into her bag, bringing out her waterbottle, sipping slowly while leaning against The Beast.

"Damn it all, Krissy. You've got to slow down and take care of yourself. It won't just be you who suffers if you don't. Baby will too."

"You think I don't know that, David?"

Krista's unaccustomed flare of temper, took them both by surprise. Deliberately sipping her water, Krista reined her temper in. Hot, tired and disappointed in her failure to unleash his memories, she had been unfair to David.

But he could have shown a bit of sympathy instead of telling me off.

"Yeah, yeah, David. I know. I'll do everything right from now on. Not that it's going to be much longer. Give me a leg up into this monster so I can sit back and relax."

David rushed to comply, and if the feel of his large, strong hands cupping her bottom made her feel more like crying than smiling, he didn't see the single tear she wiped away before pinning a cheerful smile to her lips. His worried sideways glance from the driver's seat a moment later told her she hadn't quite pulled it off.

"I'm going to have a little nap," she said, forestalling any further discussion. "Wake me up when we're home."

Adjusting her seatbelt to accommodate Baby, she closed her eyes. Moments later, what had been intended to be feigned sleep became the genuine article. Noting the change in her breathing, David eased back on the accelerator. He'd give her as much time to rest as he could.

9

"Krissy! Krissy, time to wake up, Darling. We're home."

Well, Krissy's home, David reminded himself, feeling a wistful pang that he couldn't also claim it as his. Seemed his whole life was tied up in knots waiting for the birth of Krista's baby, or the return of his memory. Whichever came first.

God, I can't stand it much longer!

He'd snapped at Krissy, the woman he loved, this afternoon, coming close to losing his temper with her. The encounter had left him feeling sick and cold inside. And inordinately scared with a fear which had seemed to be battering at him through the barrier of his amnesia. A fear which he had a gut feeling had less to do with Krissy than with what she'd once referred to as a time bomb ticking away inside him. Dread shivered through him just thinking about it.

"Mmmph." Krista mumbled unintelligibly, prising her eyelids apart and squinting at her surroundings and echoing David's words. "We're home." She sat up straighter, unclipping her seatbelt. "Already? That was quick."

David laughed, reaching up to help her down. He'd bet the drive from Hidden Cove into Townsville had set a new record for slow.

"C'mon Darling. Let's get you inside and I'll put the kettle on while you put your feet up for a bit longer."

"Sounds like a plan." Coming more wide awake each minute, Krista slid down David's body as he helped her down, ending up with her hands clasped around his neck leaning in to give him a thank-you kiss.

"Sorry I was so grumpy earlier. Put it down to the heat, my overexertion and my impatience with having to haul this huge lump around. No complaints, Baby," she gave her belly a conciliatory pat, "but I'll be really glad when I can have my body back and be myself again. Let's go get that cuppa, David Darling. It's the best offer I've had in at least half an hour."

Conversation was desultory while they sipped at their drinks, fading into silence except for Krista's murmurs of pleasure while David treated her to another of his professional standard foot massages. Tied up with her own thoughts and emotions, it took Krista a while to realise David's mood was far from upbeat, and had been since they'd arrived home.

"Darling, enough." Swinging her feet to the floor, she patted the seat beside her. "Something's bothering you. Is it something you can talk to me about?"

For a long minute she thought he wasn't going to answer, then he stood up abruptly. Striding over to the window, he stood fiddling restlessly with the cord of the vertical drapes. Krista held her peace, rewarded when he looked back at her over his shoulder.

"I feel as if pressure's building up inside me. I've felt it before. As if something's about to happen, but nothing ever does. If this is my lost memory trying to return, I wish it'd just do it and be done with it. I'm trying to get on with building a new life for myself, only I keep coming up against the bloody blockage in my mind. I feel I'm only partly here. Damn it all, Krissy, I need to know." He spun round and strode back across the room to fling himself down at her side.

"I'm going to do what you suggested, and ask Zelinka to use hypnosis to effect a breakthrough. Even though the thought of someone poking around in my mind gives me the creeps."

Laying her hand on his, Krista offered what comfort she could.

"I'm sure you're right when you say you feel a breakthrough is imminent. Today you recalled the geography of Hidden Cove perfectly, even though you had no conscious memory of it. I believe you came close. I'd tell you stuff only I don't know the dark stuff. You already have the broad outlines of what I do know, and none of that has done anything so far."

"That's the Hell of it, Krissy. Nothing helps." He hung his head, running his fingers through his hair.

After another long moment of silence, he took her hand, swinging round to face her. Krista began to feel uncomfortable under his intense gaze.

"I've never told anyone this, Krissy. No-one. Straight after I was wounded, the first time I woke up in the hospital, before I even knew I'd lost my memory, I felt there was something important I had to do." He hesitated, as if uncertain whether or not to continue.

Krista nodded, giving his hand a gentle squeeze. Holding her breath, she waited, exhaling in a silent whoosh when he began speaking again.

"It was one really vivid, clear imperative. I had to get to Townsville, asap. There was something vitally important I had to do. In Townsville. That mental command drove me to return here as soon as I could persuade the doctors it would be useful since it was the last place in Australia I'd been. Hopefully the easiest to remember. Pity it hasn't turned out that way."

He jumped to his feet and began pacing again.

"Do you have any idea what you were supposed to do when you got here?"

David shook his head.

"Not at first. After a bit, I started to think it might have something to do with you, Krissy. Especially when I learnt we had a history. I fell in love with you so fast. So deeply, I'm convinced it was because I was already in love with you from before. You said we broke up on the eve of my departure. That we had a huge falling out?"

The statement came out as more of a question. Krista nodded.

"That's right. You'd never spoken about love, or a shared future. Nothing like that at all, but I loved you and I was sure you returned my love. That you just weren't ready to say anything. Then there was the fight. Then you were gone."

"It's just my gut feeling, Darling, but I've been thinking maybe the urgent something I had to do concerned fixing things with you."

Anxiously, Krista tracked David with her eyes as he continued to pace.

"After we met, the driving compulsion to return to Townsville began to fade. Maybe because I was doing what I'd wanted desperately to do. D'you think that's at all possible? Or am I simply making events fit my own agenda?"

"It does fit, David, and I really hope it's true. If you meant to mend fences with me, before you lost your memory, that would be absolutely wonderful."

She thought about David's revelation a while longer, then decided to share something of her own with him.

"Shall I tell you something that's a rather amusing coincidence, David? It sort of bears out what you were just saying." Krista swung her legs up onto a convenient footstool she pulled into place.

"I would have told you sooner, only I hoped it might come back to you without my prompting. Only someone is bound to mention it sooner or later, so better if I tell you first."

"You're sounding very mysterious, Krissy."

David's attention was again more than half centred on Krista's long, slender legs. It had felt so good to have his hands on her, even if only for a foot massage, and he couldn't wait to do it again. A massage and more.

As well as telling him more than once she reciprocated his love in the present, now she'd confirmed their previous love affair for him, too. He and Krissy had been in love before, and he wanted that love back again. All of it, and more.

Wanted it fiercely.

Passionately.

Krista was his future; and he was determined to be hers. He was going to make a home for Krista and her baby, even though he sometimes felt ambivalent about taking on another man's child. However, the baby was part of the woman he loved. A wholly innocent part. He felt confident he was man enough to love a child for itself, regardless of its paternity.

"Not me, David. It's Fate being mysterious. Listen carefully. When we started going out together back then, you used to hitch a ride into the city with another officer who lived over on Rowes Bay. He used to drop you off near the shops and you'd walk down the street to my place in – wait for it – the Reef Gardens Apartments. How about that?"

"Reef Gardens … But …"

"I've only been in this house since just before we met up again. Guess what apartment I had at the Reef Gardens? The apartment the landlord decided to refurbish before reletting?"

Stunned, David stared at her, unable to say a word.

"You're in my old place, David. Number five. Not only that, but you furnished it almost the same as I had it."

David was frowning, trying desperately to make sense of what Krista said.

"But … How? I mean …"

"Best guess, David? I reckon you were following an unconscious memory. You were down near the shops that morning and your feet automatically took you down the street, same as they used to, ending up in the same place."

She grinned up at him.

"At a subliminal level, you must have remembered. Now is that more important than recalling the kids' birthday party?"

Closing his eyes, David breathed deeply, seeking to steady his mind which whirled out of control with a multitude of conflicting ideas jostling for supremacy. When he felt himself in control again, he sat down, close enough to take Krista's hand in his.

"It is important, Krissy. I don't remember it consciously, but Knowing it confirms so much I've been feeling. Like the sense of homecoming I felt as soon as I walked inside. It tells me something else, too. It tells me I'm right to believe I had fallen in deeply in love with you, even if, as you say, I hadn't ever spoken the words to you. Otherwise, why would your address be so strongly embedded in my subconscious?"

He raised the hand he was holding to his lips, planting a lingering kiss on Krista's palm.

"I'm right, aren't I Krissy? I loved you then, and I love you even more now. You're my forever girl. Say you'll marry me, Darling."

Whoa!

Sorely tempted to fling herself in David's arms and agree, Krista clung desperately to her more honourable convictions. Even loving him, as she was sure she did, it would be wrong to take advantage of David's ignorance of the full truth. To do so would be tantamount to entrapment.

Pushing herself into a fully upright position, she gently disengaged her hand from his clasp.

"David, I'm truly honoured that you want to marry me. You're right that we were a whole lot more than friends, although you never spoke of love back then. While I willingly admit to having very strong feelings for you, loving you, I'm not ready to make such a huge commitment. Let's wait till after Baby is born, then we can talk about the future. Please?

She was being sensible, but guilt weighed heavily on her conscience. Maybe she ought to come clean with David right now. About to, she lost the opportunity when David burst into passionate speech.

"You still don't trust me."

David's lips twisted in self-disgust.

"I can't even remember what I did, but it's still coming between us, isn't it? Can't you just tell me? Put me out of my misery so we can move on?"

He jumped to his feet, pacing her lounge room again like a cornered Tassie devil. Whirling to face her, he stood aggressively over her, hot accusations spewing from his lips.

"Or have I got it all wrong, Krissy? Maybe it was the other way round. Maybe it was *you* who hurt *me*. Is that why you're so worried about what I might remember? Did Baby's father come between us? Did you choose him over me? Is that it?"

"Absolutely not!"

Springing to her feet, Krista faced David, arms akimbo, an angry flush staining her cheeks.

Suddenly it was the old David confronting her. And she didn't like it. A cold shiver rippled down her spine.

"Then did you chuck me aside because I had to leave? That was the Army, Krista. Not me."

"That wasn't me either, you lamebrained idiot!" Krista clapped both hands over her mouth.

"Oh my God, David. That came out all wrong."

"True though. Since the explosion I really am a lamebrain. Literally. No bloody use to anyone! No wonder you're not prepared to take me on trust."

The bitterness imbuing his hushed voice tore at Krista's heart.

David flung himself down on the sofa, head in his hands. Krista knelt in front of him and peeled his hands away from his ravaged face, clasping them to her chest.

"David?" she whispered. "David, I'm so sorry. My temper got the better of me when you started making such horrible accusations. No-one else came between us. I didn't get upset because you had to do your duty. I was unhappy we'd be apart, and I was worried something bad might happen to you, but I understood, and accepted, you had no option but to go where you were sent."

She bowed her head over their clasped hands, sniffing back tears she refused to shed.

"I'd like to say 'Yes'. I really would. The only reason I'm holding back is that I want you to be fully aware of your personal history. Of who you really are, before I give you my answer." She chickened out of getting into an involved explanation that very minute. With Baby kicking her to pieces and her back aching, she simply didn't feel up to it.

"If you haven't remembered for yourself by the time Baby is born, I'll tell you everything I know and we'll take it from there. That's a firm promise," she compromised. She kissed his hands, then, releasing them, struggled awkwardly to her feet.

"I'm sorry too. I shouldn't have ripped up at you like that. Oh, Krissy. I get so frustrated with not knowing. I better go before I say anything else I shouldn't."

Locking up after biding David a disconsolate goodnight, Krista felt tears running down her cheeks. She didn't know what had just happened. He'd turned tail and left immediately, not waiting for her to see him out, with only the briefest of leave-takings. And none at all of the knee-buckling kisses and sweet words of love which had lately come to be his custom.

It had been a leave-taking eerily reminiscent of *that* one back then, only not so acrimonious.

Had the future she was dreaming of just been scuttled.

God, I hope not!

A lonely tear trickled down Krista's cheek as she took herself off to lie down.

10

Coming groggily out of a deep sleep, Krista stared blearily at her bedside clock.

Eleven thirty! Am or pm?

For a moment she was so disorientated she wasn't sure.

Pm.

The light in her room came from a streetlight, not the sun. Why hadn't she closed the blinds as she usually did? Sitting up, she groaned, clutching her stomach.

That hurt!

Wide awake now, she remembered going to lie down after David left. She must have fallen sleep.

Ugh. I'm still in the clothes I wore to the beach. And I missed dinner. I feel all hot and sweaty.

She wandered into the kitchen, detouring to the bathroom on the way for a quick comfort stop. She'd have a cool shower and put on a fresh nightie.

Followed by something to eat, she decided.

The first part of the programme was easy. Only while she stood in front of the fridge moodily surveying its contents, none of which had much appeal, another one of those pains struck. Now she was fully awake, she realised there was only one thing they could be, and it wasn't Baby kicking this time.

Braxton-Hicks or the real thing? Baby's not due till next week at the earliest. Are first babies supposed to be early or late? Doesn't matter. Either way I'm not ready yet. So, Braxton-Hicks. Gotta be.

All the same, feeling too uncomfortable for food to have any appeal, Krista slumped down on the lounge, clasping a cushion against her tummy, to have a think. According to Dr Alison Robards, her gynaecologist whom she'd seen the day before, Baby was in position and ready to come any time.

Maybe the short, sharp contractions weren't Braxton-Hicks.

Maybe they were the real thing.

"Are you coming now. Baby?" Krista rubbed her tummy gently, conversing out loud with her unborn child. "I don't think I'm ready for this, you know. How about you settle down and we wait till next week, hmmm? Grandma will be here then and we won't be all on our own."

Baby's answer was another of those short, sharp pangs. "Well, if you've made up your mind, I better get myself organised.

As she pushed herself awkwardly to her feet, there was another pain. Different. A horribly uncomfortable feeling of something giving way inside her.

As if something had ruptured.

Fearfully clutching at herself, Krista stared at the liquid trickling down her legs to pool at her feet. Petrified.

"Oh, Mum," she wailed, fighting against her fear. "Mum, I need you."

Only her mother wasn't there. Krista was on her own.

"Well," she muttered, struggling to control incipient panic. "I guess it's definitely not Braxton-Hicks." She giggled, ending in a hastily swallowed sob. "C'mon, Mallory. Hold it together, for God's sake. Baby needs you."

Seeing her phone where she'd left it the afternoon before, she picked it up and rang the number she had on speed dial for the hospital, practising some calming breaths while she waited for someone on the other end to pick up. When they did, after what seemed an interminable wait, but which in reality was no more than a few seconds, she nearly lost it.

"Oh, please," she gulped. "I think my baby's coming and I don't know what to do."

"Well, dear. You're talking to the right person. Are you booked in with us? You are. That's good. I've got all your details on our computer then. How about you tell me your name so I can bring them up. Krista Mallory. I see here you're with Dr Robards. Have you called her yet?"

Having to concentrate on answering questions helped Krista calm down. She wasn't on her own, there was a whole hospital filled with people ready, willing and able to help her. Not to mention Dr Robards.

And Lorna.

The calm friendly voice had just checked that Lorna Jansen who was listed as her birth coach would be available.

"Now that the clerical details have been checked, let's get down to the nitty-gritty, Krista. Do I need to send an ambulance for you?"

Although there had been another, slightly more prolonged contraction while she was on the phone, Krista quickly realised there was no urgency. Yet.

~~~~~

"Which bloody idiot rings at midnight, for God's sake?"

Wriggling out from beneath her husband's arm to reach for the phone, Lorna answered breathlessly.

"The kind of idiot who's in trouble."

Images of her parents, or Dan's parents in some sort of emergency situation flooded her brain, making her heart race in fear as always happened when an unexpected call woke her in the middle of the night.

"It's Krista," she said, allaying Dan's identical fears. "Krista, is it …"

"It's coming, Lorna. I really need you."

"Right with you, Kris. Sit tight."

Lorna leapt out of bed and began throwing on her clothes, dropping the phone in the process. Fortunately, it landed on the bed where Dan scooped it up.

"Lorn's getting dressed, Kris. She'll be with you in a few minutes. Hang in there."

"I'm sorry to wake you both, Dan. It's all Baby's fault. He decided he couldn't wait a day longer. Tell Lorna not to rush. I'm going to have another shower before we go in to the hospital. I rang, and they said not to be in too big a hurry as I've only just started."

"You hear that, Lorn? You can take the time to get your buttons straight. Have you called Dave, Kris? I think he wants to be in on this, doesn't he?"

Dan's question gave Krista a sinking feeling in the pit of her stomach which clashed nastily with the next contraction. They were getting more intense, she noted.

"No. No I haven't, Dan, and he did say he wanted to be with me. Guess I better call him next." A call she felt reluctant to make after their argument.

"Not to worry, Kris. Let me do it. I'll enjoy hearing him get in a panic when he gets a rude wake-up call in the middle of the night. Make up for my scare."

"Oh, Dan." Krista actually giggled. Dan's chatter was calming her almost as effectively as the nurse's had. "I really am sorry. Can you cope if Lorna doesn't get back in time for work and getting the kids to school?"

"No problems. One of the others will come in at short notice. We've had it all teed up for weeks, just in case you came early."

"Okay, then."

~~~~~

Lorna pulled into the driveway at the same time Krista finished cleaning up the puddle on the loungeroom floor.

"What are you doing?" Lorna demanded, seeing the mop in her friend's hand. "Give that here, woman. You've got more important labour to deal with than mopping the floor."

"All finished. Lucky I don't have carpet, or I'd have made a worse mess when my waters broke, but I couldn't go off and leave that mess on the floor. Now, finally, I'm going for that shower. Oooh," she concluded, another contraction beginning.

Lorna, who'd begun timing the contraction as instructed during the birthing lessons they'd attended, opened her mouth to argue the point, but taking in Krista's damp, bedraggled state, merely told her to get going. 'Keep the expectant mother calm' had been another of her instructions.

"...and look sharp about it. I want to get down to the hospital and settled in. Yell when you get the next contraction. I'm timing them."

By the time they arrived at the hospital the contractions were only five minutes apart and quite intense. Baby was obviously in rather a hurry to be born. Lorna's phone pinged to signal an incoming text.

"David's on his way," she said, steering Krista into the lift to the labour ward. "Good thing I reckon. If more men saw what we women go through in childbirth they might have a bit more respect. It's nice to be treated to gentlemanly courtesies," she rambled, deliberately trying to distract Krista, "But I really hate being treated like some dumb, helpless half-wit."

For the next few hours until Elanor Jane Mallory burst kicking and screaming into the world, they were too busy to take much notice of anything outside the delivery room.

Tired, and sweaty enough to need yet another shower, Krista looked up from besottedly inspecting fingers and toes while cooing, awestruck, at the baby in her arms. A frown flitted across her brow as she peered into the corners of the small room. Something wasn't right. Or rather, *someone* wasn't where he ought to be.

"Where's David?"

Even if he didn't understand why, he ought to be here, she though, furious at his absence. Besides, he'd promised. Was he still mad at her? Too mad to come and support her through Elanor's birth? Had all he'd said about marriage, and being a father to her baby, been wiped out by one tiny little squabble? It hadn't even been a proper fight!

"David?"

Now Lorna peered into every corner of the brightly lit room. As if an object the size of an adult male could possibly be hidden from sight in the austere delivery room.

"But … He texted me he was on his way." Lorna fiddled with her phone, switching it back on to check for messages. "He did know which hospital, didn't he?"

"I'm sure he did. Anyway, if he did end up at the wrong one, all he'd have to do would be to ring around. He'd have found us in ten minutes tops. If he wanted to." Krista sniffed, feeling close to tears.

"Now stop that, Kris. Right now. David loves you. He said he'd be here, so something must have happened to prevent him. And before you go imagining the worst, I'll see what I can do to track him down while the nurses tidy you up."

Krista watched her friend stalk off down the corridor, determination and annoyance both evident in her rigidly erect frame. Krista shivered, unconsciously tightening her hold on the baby in her arms.

~~~~~

In the hospital canteen with a rapidly cooling cup of coffee and the crumbs of a cherry Danish in front of her, Lorna worked her phone, becoming more frustrated by the minute. Why in Hell wasn't David Curtis answering his phone instead of letting it go to message bank? And why had no-one else any idea where he was? She'd even just now resorted to checking in with the police in case he'd been in a traffic accident.

How could she go back to Kris and report a total failure? Her friend needed to be relieved of her worry, not have it intensified.

Ending yet another unproductive query, Lorna flung her useless phone down on the table. Running her hands through her hair, she wondered who to try next. The Army? They'd cut him loose, weeks ago. She couldn't see anyone out at Lavarack stirring themselves.

"Excuse me."

Lorna whirled round to face the two nurses sitting at the next table.

"Hope I'm not sticking my nose in where it's not wanted, but we couldn't help overhearing." Lorna's raised brow and inclination of her head in a slow nod encouraged the nurse, the pretty blonde one, Lorna noted, to continue.

"You're trying to find someone? That sexy Army vet with amnesia?"

"Yes. He seems to have gone AWOL."

Both nurses giggled.

"Not him," the brunette older nurse snickered.

"We've got him locked down tight, right upstairs, and Sister's not letting him out till his doctor okays it. That probably won't be till later today sometime."

Lorna goggled, and opened her mouth to ask for an explanation. Blondie forestalled her.

"We had a bit of excitement last night. The cops brought in a guy high as a kite on ice. He got loose and went on a rampage. No idea what Captain Curtis was doing here at that hour, but he got in the way and ended up on the floor, out cold. The duty doc admitted him for observation, because of the concussion."

Her friend chimed in at that point, taking up the tale.

"He comes in here for physio, so we've got all his details on record. Doc Webster left a message with Curtis's own doctor. He was coming round, last we saw of him. Seemed okay, but pretty shaken up. Last we heard, it seemed the fall shook something loose, and his memory has returned. Gotta go, or we'll be late back from our break."

Telling her which ward David had been admitted to, the friendly pair waved goodbye and headed of at a fast clip.

Good news indeed, if it's true.

Well! Mission accomplished. Almost.

Feeling far more optimistic than five minutes earlier, Lorna swallowed the last of her coffee, wrinkling her nose in disgust to find it unpleasantly cold, and headed for Reception.

Who transferred her to the Charge Nurse for David's ward.

Who was very reluctant to part with any information, but who finally confirmed that Yes, David Curtis was a patient; No, he appeared physically unharmed, but that No, Lorna couldn't come to see him at such a ridiculously early hour in the morning, disturbing all the other patients on the ward. As for Lorna's query about the return of his memory, to answer that would be a breach of patient confidentiality.

Which Lorna chose to interpret as an affirmative.

Entering the lift, she punched the button for the Maternity floor. Time to report back to Krista who was probably going quietly berserk with worry by now, then, with a bit of luck, she'd be home in time to kiss her kids goodbye before they caught the bus to school.

11

"There you are!"

With a start, Krista snapped out of the doze she'd fallen into when the nurse had left her in her room. Disorientated for the moment, she blinked, her gaze darting to the transparent plastic crib alongside her bed. Relaxing when she saw Elanor sleeping peacefully and realised it wasn't her baby who'd woken her. Only then did she turn inquiring eyes towards the door.

"I've been all over this damned hospital, looking for you."

"David!" Not registering her visitor's aggressive tones, Krista smiled joyfully, pushing herself up in the bed, hands held out, welcoming him in. "I've got a little girl, David. Elanor. Like the flowers in *Lord of the Rings*. Isn't she … wonderful?"

Her voice tapered off, the fading tone indicative of anything but wonder as the man she loved stared stonily down at her, arms on hips, ignoring her greeting.

"So, Krista." David's voice was so coldly accusing it sent a shiver down Krista's spine.

"When did you plan on telling me she's mine? Or were you intending to go on leaving me in ignorance?"

Something's happened. What? What's the matter with him?

"Actually, David," Krista picked her way carefully through the minefield this confrontation had become. "I did tell you. You've just forgotten."

"Not any more. My memory's back, and I don't recall that conversation at all. Stop trying to hoodwink me with your damned lies!"

"I'm not lying, David." Krista swallowed, trying to dislodge the imaginary lump in her throat.

"I admit when we met up again and you assumed someone else was my baby's father, I went along with it," she explained. "I didn't know how to tell you the truth when you didn't even remember me. Not after the way we parted. But I really did tell you before," she repested.

"I found out I was pregnant after you'd left, so I wrote you a letter."

Knowing she had done all she could in the circumstances, she wasn't meekly taking all the blame. David had more than earned his share, and amnesia was no excuse for his present attitude.

"Letter? There was no ..." He tore at his hair. Something was niggling at the back of his mind, but he couldn't bring it to the forefront. Why couldn't he damned well recall what he needed to? When he needed to?

Krista nodded, her mind racing to keep up with him.

"I did write," she insisted.

"Oh, I get it. You got pregnant to trap me into marrying you, only that little scheme fell through when I didn't play your game. I'm surprised you didn't jump at the chance when I came back without my memory. When I'd have been putty in your hands. Pity I've got my memory back too soon, isn't it?" he sneered.

Questions rioted through Krista's mind.

So he thinks his memory is back, does he?

Where has the man I've come to know and love disappeared to?

The new improved David Curtis?

It looked like the time bomb she'd been so afraid of had just exploded, blasting him into oblivion.

Leaving her with the old version.

The one who'd repudiated her love and abandoned her, breaking her heart.

"There was no scheme!" Krista hissed defiantly. "That's all a figment of your nasty imagination. Which you'd know if you'd read my letter."

"Stop lying to me!"

Frustrated, David came up to Krista's bed in a rush and thumped his fist on her bedtable.

Krista cringed back against the pillows, anger raising red flags in her cheeks.

Elanor, startled awake, began crying.

Loudly.

"Now see what you've done!" Krista yelled, reaching out to pick up her baby.

"What's going on in here? Who are you, upsetting my mums and babies?" demanded the Charge Nurse who came bustling in at the sound of raised voices.

"I'm the baby's father, and this is a private conversation," David snapped, turning his attention back to Krista.

"A not-so-private conversation which is over. Out! I won't have you coming on my ward disturbing my patients, whoever you are." When David held his ground, looking down his nose as if addressing an insubordinate private, she added, with dangerous officiousness, "Do I need to call security?"

David wavered a moment before conceding defeat. "Okay, okay. I'm going." He turned back to Krista for one last parting shot.

"We aren't finished, Krista. You'll be hearing from me."

Just short of slamming it, he pulled the door shut behind him, striding back along the corridor the way he'd come.

Half way to the lift he realised he had company.

Lorna Jansen had fallen in on his right, matching him stride for stride.

"You blew it, didn't you Curtis?" she accused, tugging on his arm to bring him to a halt. "You went rushing in like a bull at a gate, not stopping to think anything through or make sure you had the facts straight, and you blew it. Big time."

Krista was beyond his reach, so David turned on her friend who was not so fortunate.

"She lied to me, Lorna. Just like you, and everyone else, did. Thinking because I'd lost my memory you could palm me off with any old story. Well, you can't! That's my baby, and no-one's going to keep her from me!"

He glared at Lorna as if expecting her to refute his accusation. To return aggression with aggression. Instead, she looked as if she was holding back laughter. So not the reaction he expected.

"No-one's trying to keep her from you, so calm down. For God's sake, Curtis," Lorna breathed in, controlling the betraying quiver of her lips. "Even I, with no medical knowledge whatsoever, could have predicted your memory wouldn't return in a neatly organised package. I bet it's all mixed up in a confusing jumble. Bits of this and that popping up out of sequence all over the place."

David glared at her some more, refusing to acknowledge just how accurately she'd called it.

"It is, isn't it?"

No-one could shut Lorna Jansen up when she knew she was in the right.

"Question is, what are you going to do about the mess you've gone and got yourself into with Krista? I'd take a bet she's not talking to you after the ruckus I overheard as I arrived just now."

"She shouldn't have lied to me Lorna. She even insisted she'd told me about the baby." With no-one else remotely on his side, David poured out his grievances, whether Lorna wanted to hear them or not.

"Said she wrote me a letter. Hah! I never got any damned letter from her!"

His head ached, and that disturbing niggle was still there, only now it felt like something screaming to get out. He wished it would shut up and leave him alone.

Lorna pursed her lips, contemplating how much to reveal. She was sticking her oar into something that, strictly speaking, wasn't any of her business. But Krista was her best friend. She nodded to herself, decision made.

"Actually, David," To the beleaguered male in front of her she sounded almost sympathetic. "After she found out she was pregnant, Kris did write to you. About two months after you shipped out. And you did receive the letter. It was sent registered mail, so there's a record of delivery. Before you talk to Krista again, you better remember what you did with that letter. It's important." And that was as much as she was prepared to say. Almost.

"One more thing, David." Lorna paused to be certain he was listening.

"You better do some serious thinking about what you want from Krista before you make things even worse. Talk to me if you need someone to listen. Krista's my friend, but as long as there's no conflict of interests I can be your friend too. A better friend than you deserve."

Surprising both herself and him, Lorna threw her arms around the stubborn idiot in a bearhug that had him hugging her back, eyes tight shut against the tears gathering behind his lids.

"Now, get going back to wherever you escaped from, and start thinking before you act. I'll just look in on Krista, then I'm off home. Bye, Curtis."

David stood gazing at Lorna's rapidly retreating back, feeling he'd been caught in a whirlwind. Had Krista really been telling him the truth? If she had ...?

Lorna was right.

He'd blown it.

Big time.

David became aware his head was pounding so hard he felt dizzy. The doctor who'd seen him during the night had warned him about the after-effects of severe concussion. He could barely put one foot ahead of the other in a straight line as he reluctantly made his way back to the ward he'd snuck out of half an hour earlier.

It felt defeatist, but he needed to lie down.

Before he fell down.

FORGOTTEN

12

Looking up on hearing a tentative knock at the door, Krista saw David Curtis waiting for permission to enter.

A very subdued, even sheepish, David Curtis.

Well! If he thinks he can just come crawling back and everything will be the same, he can think again.

"*Now* what do you want?"

David flinched at Krista's surliness.

"Krista!" The older woman sitting beside the bed sounded scandalised.

"Where are your manners? That's no way to welcome visitors."

"Maybe he's not welcome, Mum."

Krista hadn't taken her eyes off David, not for one second, and noted with satisfaction that he blanched at her words.

Had a change of heart, has he?

Good!

Then she remembered Lorna's visit early that morning. Her best friend had advised her not to let her temper push her too far. To cut David Curtis some slack when he came crawling back as she was certain he would. Said she'd talked some sense into the stupid idiot.

All well and good, but he can do some crawling first, Krista thought vindictively, still smarting from his unfair accusations during his dawn raid.

He'd caught her off guard, knowing nothing about his memory returning. Which she wasn't entirely convinced of since he didn't remember her letter. She'd been worried sick by his non-appearance, and had been so glad to see him safe and well.

Until he launched his verbal assault. She'd never been so pleased to see anyone as she had been when the Charge Nurse sailed in and chucked him out.

"Don't just stand there," she said, not relenting an inch, but willing to give him a chance to prove himself. One way or the other.

"You might as well come in. As long as you can be civil."

Krista felt totally justified in her own incivility. Her mother, sensing the deep conflict between her daughter and the man she was giving such a hard time, kept her thoughts to herself.

"I came to apologise," David said, glancing uncertainly at the stranger who'd reprimanded Krista's breach of good manners.

Apologise?

Krista's mother, agog with curiosity, avidly followed the exchanges back and forth between David and Krista.

"Yes, Mum. This is David Curtis, and he sure as Hell owes me an apology. David, this is my mother, Jane Mallory. David is Elanor's father," she added for her mother's benefit.

"Oh!" Jane's lips twitched, comprehension dawning. She took the hand David held out, giving it a sympathetic squeeze.

"Nice to meet you at last, David. This apology sounds as if it ought to be delivered in private. I'll just go and find your father, Krista, and we'll take our coffee elsewhere."

She patted David on the shoulder and waved him into the chair she hurriedly vacated, but he chose to perch on the edge of her bed instead, wanting to be as close to Krista as he could get.

"Dad was transferred to Mackay a couple of years ago, and he and Mum drove up early this morning. They arrived a little while ago," Krista said, then, inhaling deeply, tackled the issue between them.

"I'm listening, David. Please don't shout. Elanor has only just dropped off after meeting her grandparents."

"Wasn't intending to shout," he mumbled.

Wistfully, David stared into the crib. He dearly wanted to meet his daughter himself, but he needed to make his peace with her mother first.

Bracing himself, he gathered his courage, looked Krista firmly in the eye, and ... forgot every last word of his prepared spiel. Panic threatening, he blurted out the first words that came to his lips.

"I love you Krissy. I ... Damn it all, that's not what I meant to say. I ..."

"You mean you *don't* love me?"

Cutting him some slack was one thing, but she wasn't going to make it easy for him.

"No. I mean yes. I do love you, only I meant to tell you I'm sorry about this morning." Mentally cursing his ineptitude, David ran his fingers through his hair and began again.

"I was way out of line, coming here, going off at you. What I said then came out all wrong too. I was going to be calm and reasonable and just ask you to explain. Help me sort out the bits I recalled that were confusing me. Only, first I couldn't find you, then when I did find you, looking so impossibly beautiful and happy when I felt like crap, I lost it. It felt like another betrayal, and I ..."

He ran his fingers through his hair again, rubbed at his eyes, and looked at Krista in mute despair.

She waited.

Sounded as if Lorna had been spot-on with her take, but somehow, Krista felt David had to actually put his feelings into words. For his own sake. She nodded encouragingly. And waited some more while he disappeared inside his mind searching for the truth contained in his memories. Trying to line them up in order.

"I blew it this morning, didn't I? Big time. Now, when I'm trying to put it right nothing's coming out the way I planned it. I'm sorry, Krissy."

She couldn't stand it. Not a moment longer. The poor dope needed a hand if they were to progress beyond saying he was sorry.

"Look, David," Krista struggled against her impatience. "Let's agree you're sorry. What I want to know is why you immediately jumped to such a nasty conclusion? Why did you dump me in the first place? Why did you send such a horrible reply when I wrote to you? What's all this talk of betrayals?"

I didn't betray him, so who did? And how? Was it Sharon? His mother? Someone else I've never heard of?

Anger, on David's behalf, no longer aimed at him, began to stir in Krista's breast.

David looked at her, aghast, the memories whirling in his brain like giant birds. Beating, beating at him with their wings, harder with every question.

"Stop! Stop! I can't keep up!" He clapped his hands over his ears and squeezed his eyes tight shut.

"Okay." Krista reached out, putting her arms around him and pulling him down onto her breast. "Shhh." She rubbed his back, feeling his breath steadying gradually. Finally he sat back up, looking at her through anguished eyes.

"I thought when my memory returned, that would be it. Everything back where it ought to be. Seems it doesn't work that way, at least not for me. It's all there, Krissy, accessible if I know the right question to ask. Only I'm not sure I do."

"This sounds almost as complicated as running around all over Townsville trying to spark memories the way we've been doing."

"Not quite. Can we take it one question at a time?"

"For sure, Darling."

"You called me Darling. Does that mean you're giving me another chance, Krissy? In spite of all my stuff-ups?"

What a no-brainer.

Miraculously, the David Krista liked best was back, remembering he loved her and finally willing and able to talk about his past. If only she could hold onto him, keeping his other persona at bay. She crossed her fingers out of his sight.

"Well, of course. I love you, you idiot. I've always loved you, practically from the very beginning. Do you remember how we met?"

Somehow, having Krista call him an idiot sounded like the most loving, reassuring endearment David had ever heard. A wobbly smile curled his lips up at the corners. If Krissy loved him, he could conquer all his problems, and then some.

"That's an easy one. Course I do. I was furious at being ordered to babysit some smart-aleck female writer who looked so damn cute my guts were tying themselves up in knots. I didn't know how I'd get through a whole week watching you being fawned over by all those sex-starved soldiers."

Feeling more confidant, he leaned forward, claiming her smiling lips in a kiss that tied Krista's guts up in knots.

And more.

"Krissy, I've thought about all the things I said this morning. You really were telling the truth, weren't you? I had everything the wrong way round. It wasn't you betraying me; it was *me* who betrayed *you*."

"Finally!" Krista huffed, exasperated.

"I didn't tell you about Elanor when you came back because I didn't want to put undue pressure on you. Other than that, I haven't lied, David. Maybe I haven't always told the whole truth, but I've never actually outright lied."

Relief rippled across his face. In his mind he was already separating Krista from those women who'd soured his view of all women.

He could trust Krista. He would. A smile lit up his face, and he kissed her again for luck.

"One last question, Krissy, for now at least. I've thought about this, and I don't understand how you got pregnant."

Krista smirked, eyebrow raised.

"Darling," she murmured, almost laughing at the colour flooding David's face, "If you don't know that by now …"

"But you were on the pill," he stoically stuck to his guns.

Krista relented.

"I was, and believe me, it was a huge surprise for me, too. When I asked my doctor, I was astounded at the failure statistics for the pill. Failures that can't be medically explained. She said I was just one of the unlucky ones. Or lucky, depending on your point of view."

Warm and loving, her gaze strayed to the baby snoozing in the crib beside her bed.

Lucky. Definitely lucky.

David turned his eyes in the same direction, a similar expression filling them.

"Krissy, now we're on the same page at last," David whispered, his eyes remaining fixed on the crib with its precious contents, "what I really, really want to do before we go any further, is say hello to my daughter. Do you mind?"

"I'd mind more if you didn't want to," Krista whispered back, "but first …" The kiss she gave him was for more than luck. It was a pledge to their future. Guaranteed to make his toes curl.

"Ahem!" The interrupting cough was accompanied by a brisk rat-a-tat on the open door. "Enough of that, people. This is a hospital, not your bedroom at home."

Both blushing hotly, David and Krista let go, David rising to stand behind the chair, holding tightly to its back. Was he about to be evicted again?

"Brought you a roomie, Kris." Gianna, the nurse who'd been in and out of the room all morning winked, and wheeled her new patient over to the vacant bad across from Krista. "This is Sandra. She had a little boy this morning."

While Sandra was being installed in her bed, Krista's parents, back from their coffee break and eager to discover how what they fervently hoped was a reconciliation, was going, peeked around the door.

Resigning herself to postponing all the questions she still longed to ask, Krista waved them in and introduced David to her father, Tom Mallory.

With any opportunity for private conversation gone, she smiled ruefully up at David, offering the ultimate in forgiveness.

"Wanna cuddle the princess?"

Did he ever!

13

Among the steady stream of visitors coming and going through Krista's hospital room, leaving cards, flowers and gifts in their wake, David was the most constant. His gorgeous, dark red Mr Lincoln roses and chocolate-brown teddy in plaid waistcoat and pink bow-tie were awarded pride of place on top of the bedside locker.

After meeting Krista's parents the first morning, David had stayed only long enough to fall under the spell of his infant daughter. Reluctantly easing Elanor gently back into her crib, he'd stood up and made his farewells.

"I've gotta go, Krissy. Dr Zelinka said I should call him as soon as my memory returned. When I did today, he said my confusion and headaches were to be expected, and slotted me in for an emergency appointment late this morning. I'm going to be upfront with him about everything. Hopefully he'll be able to help."

"I'm sure he will, Darling." When he'd hesitated, glancing sidelong at her parents on the other side of her bed, she'd tugged him down, kissing him soundly.

They hadn't had time to talk, but she'd made her decision and his words just now merely confirmed it for her.

Her parents could start getting used to seeing them as a couple. Especially her father who had to get back to work. Meeting the man who'd wronged his daughter, he'd looked a bit grim. She planned to have a long chat with her mother who was the more flexible of the two.

~~~~~

For as long as Krista remained in the hospital there'd been no time for the complicated, intimate conversations she and David needed so urgently to have. Therefore, they'd agreed to put all discussions about their future on hold until they could be assured of their privacy; which meant until Krista and Elanor were home.

Back in her own bed, Krista had just settled down to give Elanor her early morning feed when her phone pinged, signalling an incoming message.

David.

Ring me when you get a moment, he'd texted. She'd teased him once about his refusal to use text abbreviations, but, smiling, she had to admit it was nice to know exactly what he said without translation. Made even his most mundane communications seem special.

"Shall we ring your Daddy right now, Ellie? He's texting, so we know he's awake." A rhetorical question since she had already hit the call button and had the phone up to her ear, pursing her lips to greet him with kissy noises when he answered.

Always ready to encourage ordinary, normal behaviour in him, she'd noticed how he'd loosened up on his once strict adherence to a no-nonsense approach to life. And romance.

"God, Krissy. I wish I was there with you," he responded, receiving her phone-kiss. "How was our girl's first night in her own home?"

Our girl. I do like the sound of that.

Krista smiled.

"Good. Really good. It's so much more peaceful here than in the hospital. You know, I wish you were here with me too. Both of us do, in fact. Ellie's up with me for early breakfast."

It was nice chatting to David while her daughter suckled enthusiastically at her breast, but there was a tension in his voice which told her this was more than a simple morning call. She could have strung it out a bit longer, but took pity on him and gave him an opening to get down to business.

"You're calling early, David."

"I need to see you. Soon. I've got a lot to catch you up on, Krissy Darling, and I knew Elanor would have you awake at dawn. I've got things to do this morning, so can I come over this afternoon?"

"Sure. Why not come for lunch? Mum's stocked the fridge for me, so there's plenty to go round. Dan brought me a fresh coral trout, if you like fish."

"Irresistible. My two favourite girls and coral trout as well." The lilt in his voice told Krista he was smiling.

"I'll be there."

"Think you'd better make that three girls. Mum will be here too. I'll ask her to give us some privacy after lunch so we can talk."

~~~~~

Accordingly, giving an approving nod to David who'd begun clearing the table and stacking the dishwasher without prompting, Jane Mallory yawned ostentatiously.

"I think I'll just go and have a lie down with Bronwyn Parry. Have you read her latest, Krista?" Picking up *The Clothier's Daughter* from the end table, she showed it to her daughter.

"No, I haven't, and I want to."

"I'll let you have it when I'm finished." With that, Jane padded off down the hall to the guest bedroom. She hoped they sorted themselves out soon, she was getting tired of absenting herself.

Clean-up done, Krista collected a jug of iced tea, glasses and the baby monitor.

"C'mon Darling. Let's go sit by the pool," she invited, leading the way into the back garden.

Solicitously settling Krista on one of the pair of sun-loungers on her pool deck, David poured her a glass of iced tea then fussed with the umbrella until it was at the perfect angle.

Actions Krista impatiently recognised for the delaying tactics they were. Finally, with no more distractions to fall back on, he sat on the side of his sun-lounge, head down and hands clasped, white-knuckled between his knees.

He'd made it through lunch, relying heavily on good manners and Elanor's presence to avoid being drawn into a personal conversation, however, the hard talk couldn't be deferred indefinitely.

He'd asked for the chance to clear the air. It was what he'd come for today, and he owed it to Krista to be scrupulously honest with her.

This time round.

Unlike the first time. He cringed inwardly recalling his earlier treatment of her, every nuance of which he now recalled with terrifying clarity.

He couldn't accept the future she'd so generously offered unless she knew the truth about him. That really would be a betrayal of the very worst kind. But it was so much harder than he'd anticipated.

Taking his courage in his hands, he lifted his eyes to hers and opened his mouth.

A split second longer, and Krista, already beginning to fidget, would have lost patience and begun bombarding him with questions.

"Krissy Darling, ..." David's voice wavered to a halt. He began again. Voice firmer. Determined to admit his faults, difficult as doing so would be.

"Krissy, I've remembered everything. With Zelinka's help, I think I've got it straight in my mind, and I'm utterly appalled at how badly I treated you last year. Now I understand why you were so reluctant to have anything to do with me when I came back. Oh, Krissy, I'm so very, very sorry."

He dropped his head into his hands, muffling his next words, but Krista was certain she heard correctly.

"I really thought I was doing what was best for you."

Best for me?

Best for me?

Krista stared at David's bowed head. Pain, born of unresolved, past hurts awakened and rose to the surface from where she'd buried them, metamorphosed into anger. A volcano building pressure. About to erupt.

Best for me?

Rage over-rode her earlier resolution to hear him out and make a reasoned, and reasonable, response. She jumped to her feet, towering over him, hands planted firmly on her hips.

"How could it possibly be '*best for me*' to be used? Treated as a sex toy. Of no importance. '*Best for me*' to be emotionally abused? '*Best for me*' to have my love and trust betrayed?"

The words spewed violently from her mouth, sending David reeling back.

"You explain that to me, David Curtis, because I can't see any way what you did can be excused, let alone how any of what you did can be construed as being '*best for me*'! '*Best for me?*' No way, David! No way!"

When amnesia had blocked his memory of his actions, she'd been able to forgive; only that amnesty no longer applied.

Abruptly, her knees gave way. Still in the grip of relentless fury, she slumped onto the edge of her lounger, facing David, practically knee-to-knee.

Fists clenched in her lap. Lips closed so tightly they lost every vestige of colour. Eyes ablaze. Krista blinked away tears, refusing to allow herself to weaken.

Last time she'd been blind-sided. Stunned. Totally beyond response, she'd listened to him deliver the death knell to her hopes and dreams for a happy future. Watched him shrug his shoulders and calmly walk out the door. Out of her life. Supposedly for ever.

Not this time.

Fate had given them a second chance.

Given *her* a second chance to hold David accountable for his actions. And she was in no mood to be fobbed off with mealy-mouthed platitudes.

Krista waited him out.

Waited, and watched expressions of horror, guilt, fear and finally, resolution, chase each other across a face open today as she'd never seen it in the past.

FORGOTTEN

14

Breathing deeply, David reined in his stampeding emotions. For the first time he understood the enormity of his behaviour. The terrible blow he'd dealt Krista. Krista whom he'd loved then, and now wanted for his forever love. His wife. He struggled for words to explain himself.

The words weren't there. His mind had gone blank again, but explain he must. And would.

Clutching at straws he decided to start with his last session with Dr Henry Zelinka. His shrink. He swallowed. And swallowed again, moistening his desert-dry mouth.

"I'll try to explain." He sounded unutterably feeble, even to himself. What his weak, shaky words sounded like to Krista he could only imagine.

"I'm not making excuses. There are no excuses, Krissy."

You've got that right! Krista's lips tightened even further.

"I'm just trying to explain so you'll understand," David continued, on a roll now he'd finally got started.

"You said once you believed there was something bad in my past. Something I'd never shared with you, which made me the selfish, inconsiderate bastard who hurt you back then. You were right, Krissy."

He risked a quick glance to gauge her reaction. So far, so good. She was listening, her posture fractionally less rigid.

"I talked to Zelinka about the things I remembered. Childhood stuff, and some later incidents, which I believed had made me the up-tight, dysfunctional idiot I was when I met you. His words, Krissy. He agreed with me, and we're going to work through those issues. It's going to take time for me to come to terms with it all, but he says the process can't be rushed through if we want the best results."

Another glance.

Another nod.

"I didn't go into detail, but when I told him how I'd broken it off with you, he agreed with me that I should talk to you. He said, if I wanted you in my life, then I had to tell you everything. And I do, Krissy. Want you in my life, that is. I love you."

The last words were a cry from his heart. The truth.

Truth to ease the pain in Krista's own heart.

She nodded to herself, then told him to go on. The fire burning in her eyes had softened to yearning.

"Yes. Well."

David took a minute to gather his thoughts, his hands clenched into white-knuckled fists. He was about to reveal the truth behind his appalling behaviour last year.

It didn't come easy.

Watching, Krista felt a savage satisfaction. She was glad this was hard for him. Easy would have belittled her heartbreak.

"Briefly, Krissy, my father was a sadistic brute who used to beat up my Mum, and later me too if I crossed a line that changed by the hour. I never felt safe, and as I got older his punishments escalated from a whack around the legs to a real beating. Mum had long since passed the point of being able to protect me. She couldn't even protect herself."

Wordlessly, Krista moved to sit by his side, her hand reaching across to gently cover his.

Whatever she'd imagined, it wasn't this.

David turned her hand over, clasping it tightly. Grateful for the lifeline. The support. The understanding. Did it mean what he hoped it did? Did Krissy love him, or was it merely her compassionate nature coming to the fore? Even half as much as he loved her would be enough. If she loved him. Strengthened by hope, he continued his story.

"Then, one day I came home from school and Mum was gone. He hit the bottle. Blamed everything on me. Gave me a worse beating than ever. Usually he was careful not to leave marks where they showed, but that time he was so mad he forgot. He was in a drunken stupor when I left for school the next day, barely able to drag myself to the bus top. Teacher took one look at me and raised the roof. I ended up in care and him in jail. Died there."

He shrugged, but Krista read beneath the surface, imagining how she'd have felt if it had been her father.

"I don't know what happened to Mum," David continued. "Never saw her again. I'm afraid I blamed her. Probably unjustly, but if she'd done the sensible thing and run the first time he hit her, taking me with her, life would have been a whole lot different. For both of us."

He felt Krista's arm slip around him. Hugging him tightly.

"Joined the Army when I left school. I liked the security of it. The order. Always knowing where I stood. Do my job and everything was fine. I'd been forever getting into fights at school, but the Army gave me a legitimate outlet for my aggression. I wasn't much good socially, but the fights stopped. Life was the best it had ever been."

He paused, glancing uncertainly at Krista as he recalled she had never been particularly enamoured of Army life. In fact, she'd been downright scathing on more than one occasion, reinforcing the belief he held then that there was no place for her in his future.

"I get that, David. I sort of got it back then, too. Although not knowing your background, while I respected your commitment to your career, I couldn't see why an intelligent, capable man with so many options available to him, needed such strict regimentation in his life. You've had it worse than I imagined."

"I'm not finished."

No, he's not, she realised. *He hasn't even touched on us.*

"Go on, then."

"Okay. Then there was Sharon."

Krista's heart sank. Did she really want to know about the other woman he'd loved?

No choice. Sharon was part of David's life. An important part, obviously. She gritted her teeth, holding back her opinion formed from what Kate had told her of David's ex-fiancée.

Oblivious to Krista's inner conflict, David ploughed on.

"You told me you'd heard about an ex-fiancée. That was her. Sharon King. She couldn't accept that the Army had first call on my time. Wanted me out. Came home from an overseas deployment and discovered she'd betrayed me every way possible."

Replaying Kate Wilson's more detailed revelations in her mind, Krista's fury boiled up inside her again. Fury at the woman who'd selfishly caused so much damage. Not at David. Not any more. For him she felt only compassion. And love.

"When I confronted her, all the rage inside me erupted. I wanted to smash her face in. Make her sorry for what she'd done. Scared the Hell out of me. Felt I was no better than my old man. Later, I did some reading, and discovered domestic violence is passed down from one generation to the next in a self-perpetuating cycle. Horrific stuff when you apply it to yourself. When it's who you are."

He scrubbed his hands over his face.

Krista couldn't be certain, but she'd swear she heard a muffled sob. She felt sick to the stomach herself. David had lived this horror story.

She had to force herself to go on listening when he continued.

"After Sharon, I steered clear of girls because I was afraid of what I might do some day. Then I met you, Krissy."

David turned his anguished gaze onto Krista, mutely beseeching her to understand.

Silent tears tracked down her cheeks. She tried to dredge up an encouraging smile, failing dismally when her lips wobbled with suppressed sobs. A squeeze of his hand had to suffice.

"You knocked me for six the moment I saw you. You were special, but I knew I ought to keep my distance, and I tried, Krissy. I really did. Until that night you danced with me and drove me back to the Base. I couldn't resist kissing you, and then I was lost. I kept telling myself I wouldn't keep our date. You know, the kids' birthday party?"

Krista nodded. She remembered it well, as she did every single one of their dates.

Nothing wrong with my memory.

"Kept telling myself I'd cancel. Right up till you opened your door, and I weakened. After that, I changed my tune. Told myself we were just friends. When I shipped out our affair would come to a natural end. Until then I stored up memories. And denied I was in love with you. Refused to believe you were in love with me. Breaking off with you, leaving you, was the hardest thing I'd ever done, but I had no option, Krissy. Not if I was going to protect you from the demon inside me. And I had to."

Again, Krista was glad it had been hard for him. She felt it validated her continuing love for him.

"That's why I wrote that awful reply without even reading your letter when you wrote to tell me you were having my baby."

Eyes pleading for forgiveness, David looked up at Krista.

This time Krista couldn't hold the sobs back. What he termed 'that awful reply' to her letter had finally destroyed the last tiny hope she had of a reconciliation. With it, she'd accepted he was the no-good bastard Lorna had begun referring to him as.

"I remembered your letter, and what I did with it, Krissy. After I'd had time to rest. And think quietly. I'm so sorry." His words were apologetic, but his tone was excited. Eager. There was a sparkle in his eyes all of a sudden.

Puzzled, Krista stared at him in mute appeal.

"The good thing is, Krissy, remembering the letter led me to recall why it was so important I get back to Townsville."

David's voice was triumphant.

"It was because of your letter. It kept me awake at night, ashamed for not reading it. Wondering if I'd lost my last chance at happiness. Because, Krissy, you'd been keeping me awake ever since I left you. I'd hardly been top of my game, but at last I had it figured out my big mistake had been breaking up with you. I finally admitted to myself that I loved you. That you were my hope for the future. The day the bomb exploded, I'd decided to try to call you when we got back to Base. To beg you to give me another chance. That was the important task waiting for me here in Townsville."

David wrapped both arms around Krista, holding her against his shoulder as new tears flowed down her cheeks. Tears through which her smile held the radiance of a rainbow.

"I would have agreed," she whispered. "I would have given you a second chance."

David watched her wipe her eyes and scrub her wet cheeks with a tissue, unsure if he should keep going with his story or not. Krista was happy now. Could they leave it at that? Even as he asked the question, David knew they couldn't.

Dr Zelinka had said he should get all the impediments to their happiness out in the open, and not leave anything to fester away unseen to cause problems down the track.

"David?" Krista half whispered noticing his change of mood.

What more is there?

Mentally, Krista backtracked the conversation to the point where David had diverged to tell her about remembering the letter.

Back to where he'd told her he dumped her to protect her from himself. From his violent inner demons. That was it, she realised. The reason for the whole sorry mess lay in his belief he was a danger to her. And to Ellie. Determined to get to the bottom of it, she stiffened her spine. Sat up straight.

David's nerves jittered, but he resolutely held her gaze.

"David," Krista claimed his attention. Not that it had strayed in the slightest degree. "What you said about breaking up with me? That it was because you were afraid if we stayed together, you'd hurt me the way your father hurt your mother?"

David nodded, misery too strong for words.

"But … I need to be sure, here, David. When you confronted Sharon, did you really hit her the way you said you wanted too?"

She was relieved when he jerked back, flinging his head up as if she'd slapped him.

"No." Then, realising that single clipped denial wasn't enough, he added, "I had my fist up, drawn back to hit her, but when I threw the punch, I pulled it at the last moment and slammed my fist into the wall beside her instead. Then I hightailed it out of there before I had a second go at her."

"Have you ever hit any woman?"

"Never!"

If it hadn't been such a deadly serious matter, she'd have laughed at the affronted expression on his face. His sheer repugnance lifted her spirits.

"So, let me get this straight. You've never actually hurt anyone? It's just that you're afraid you might? Because of what your father was?"

"Yes. But Krissy, it's a legitimate fear, given my family history."

"I agree. I've researched the subject for my books. Only, David, what I've learned is that if someone is really determined, and gets the right help, they can break the cycle."

"I'm determined, Krissy. And Dr Zelinka is willing to work with me. You and Elanor are the incentive I needed to push me into asking for help. I love you both. I want to marry you and be a father to Elanor. But now I know about my past, I want to be sure I can be a man who protects his family, not the poor excuse for a human being my father was. Zelinka says we should treat it as a type of mental illness, sort of like PTSD. Even if you say there's no hope of us being a family, I'm going to do it for myself. I can understand you might think me too great a risk, especially after what I've already done to you."

"Shush!"

Laying her fingers across his lips, Krista finally managed to smile.

"It's a horrible story, Darling. You've had a horrible life. But you know what? I admire you for facing up to your demons. For talking and bringing them out into the open. I believe you've got the strength of character to defeat them, and if I can help, I will. I want to, because I love you, too. I want to marry you, too. As soon as you feel you're ready."

"Yes!"

Surging to his feet, David hauled Krista up with him, whirling her round and round. Slowing to a halt, he let her slide down his body till her feet touched ground. His lips had barely claimed hers when a piercing wail sent them springing apart.

"Ellie," Krista exclaimed, recovering first and reaching for the baby monitor to switch it off. She reached for David's hand, lacing their fingers together.

"Come along Daddy. Time for your first lesson in changing your daughter's nappy. Or are you going to wimp out?" She raised a brow, laughter at the ready. In truth, she was glad of the interruption after the tension of the previous hour. She felt a little giddy. Lightheaded.

"I guess it's part of the whole parenting deal, isn't it?" David agree, grimacing at the thought of cleaning up after the baby.

"We've got her, Mum," Krista called, seeing her mother peep out the guest room door, "but I reckon a cup of tea is just what we all need right now, if you don't mind putting the kettle on."

Hands that could strip and reassemble a gun, blindfolded, were less nimble with sticky tabs, but David managed a creditable result with his first nappy change.

"At least it stayed in place," Krista laughed, settling into the comfortable feeding chair and putting Elanor to her breast. "My brother Todd's first time, it fell off as he picked my baby nephew up. Thanks, Mum," she looked past David to where her mother carried in a tea tray through the nursery door. "But there's no need for room service. David could have fetched it. Please, join us. We've got a few things to share with you."

As Jane was about to sit down, the phone in her pocket rang.

"Your father, Kris," she said, looking at the screen. "I'll take my tea to the other room while I talk to him."

"Tell him David and I are engaged," Krista called after her. Startled, Jane hesitated, then with a broad grin, hurried out.

"Tom, you'll never guess ..."

Krista heard as her mother pattered off down the hallway. Chuckling softly, she looked across at David, who looked even more startled by her announcement.

"Are we Krissy? Engaged, I mean?"

"Well I certainly reckon we are. You said you want to marry me. I replied in the affirmative. That makes it official, don't you think?"

David's grin rivalled the tropical sun shining through the window.

"Yes!"

He dropped to his knees beside the low chair where she sat with Elanor, folding them both into his embrace, kissing Krista. It wasn't much of a kiss as his daughter made no bones about voicing her displeasure at being disturbed in the middle of her meal. They both laughed rather breathlessly as they drew far enough apart not to crush the baby between them.

"Krissy, that's wonderful. Just absolutely bloody wonderful. Only …" David hesitated to mention the doubt suddenly assailing him. "Didn't we agree to wait till I've got myself sorted out?"

"Ummm. Sure. But is there any reason we can't make a commitment to each other now, with an engagement, and set the date later?"

Krista frowned, wondering if she was being too pushy, but she needn't have worried. David's blinding grin flashed again. The man literally radiated happiness.

She knew there were likely to be setbacks ahead, but Krista was confident they'd win through in the end since now they were working together to set David free from his ugly past.

15

In the end, their engagement wasn't so very long.

David made excellent progress, and when Krista invited him to move in with her so they could be a proper family for Elanor, he agreed, suggesting they get married first.

"I can do this Krissy. No way I'll backslide with you supporting me. Let's just get married."

Only too happy to agree, Krista, who'd been quietly making her arrangements for the casual, tropical wedding she preferred, swung into action.

A month from the day they were granted a marriage licence, on the last Saturday in October, Tom Mallory escorted his daughter to where David waited with the marriage celebrant, Lorna's older sister, Julie Kowalski, under a shady tree on The Strand. The same tree they had climbed on their first date, and which featured in one of David's earliest returning memories.

Mother Nature, in benign mood, turned on a perfect cool, sunny Spring afternoon.

A host of close family and friends sat in a broad semi-circle behind him, leaving an aisle through the middle for Krista to make her entrance, preceded by a flock of children – her two nieces and nephew and the Jansen twins. When asked if she was sure she wanted them all as attendants, Krista had just laughed.

"It's a family occasion, Lorna. Let them enjoy being part of it. They're more likely not to get up to mischief if they feel important, don't you think."

Krista's sister-in-law, Siobhan, who was married to her brother Todd, stood with her as matron of honour. David, with no family to call on, invited Brian Wilson to be his best man.

Brian, resigning from the Army on his return to Australia, had moved his family to Townsville where he and Kate had become firm friends with David and Krista. Friends and business partners, Brian joining David in his adventure-ecotourism venture. With his financial input they now had two Troop-carriers being prepared to take paying guests on personalised expeditions. They were due to lead their first tour group up into the Bellenden-Kerr Ranges at the beginning of December. The partnership had the added bonus of Kate working as their booking agent, keeping it all in the family.

Behind the official wedding guests stood more than twice as many casual passers-by attracted by the balloons, streamers and music. It was a good-natured crowd who cheered when Julie pronounced David and Krista man and wife, inviting David to kiss his bride.

Even the bridal couple's infant daughter, safe and snug in her grandmother's arms, cooed and clapped her tiny, pudgy hands.

Adjourning to a nearby resort hotel for the reception, they danced the evening away till the band called it quits, retiring to a suite upstairs after the ritual tossing of the bouquet.

Kim Lawrence, the corporal who had served in David's unit, cast a blushing glance at her escort, a recent North Queensland Cowboys recruit, when the neatly tied bunch of flowers landed in her arms.

The next morning David and Krista collected Elanor from her grandparents who'd minded her for the night, and caught the ferry across to Magnetic Island. A place holding none but the happiest of memories for both of them, with more to be added.

THE END

I hope you enjoyed reading
Forgotten

Please turn the page for a preview of Lena West's new

Oxley Crossing Romance,

The Making of Joey Lambert

Here is Your Preview of

The Making of Joey Lambert

A Contemporary Australian Romance by

LENA WEST

1

"Stop! Gwyneth, stop!"

Joey Lambert swung round on hearing the shouting to see a young girl dashing after a soccer ball which was rolling out onto Bridge Street, the main road through Oxley Crossing. Closer than the woman doing the shouting, he instinctively raced forward, grabbing a fistful of the girl's shirt a split second before she ran in front of a semi-trailer. The driver gave a blast on his horn, and a thumbs up to Joey as he roared by.

"My ball!" wailed the girl as she was hauled back onto the footpath and released.

"Gwynna! You nearly got skittled by that truck. Your ball's not that important." Flinging herself to her knees, the slight, blonde woman clutched the girl, Gwyneth, tightly against her chest, looking gratefully up, way up, into Joey's chocolate-brown eyes, her own brimming with tears.

"Thank you, Mister." Her voice shook, and she sucked in a deep breath before continuing. "Thank you so much. My Gwynna mightn't realise how close an escape she had, but I do."

A brief, radiant smile bloomed as she stood, tilting her head to look up at her daughter's saviour, a man head and shoulders taller than her meagre one hundred and fifty-seven centimetres.

"My pleasure, Ma'am." Joey blushed to the roots of his mop of overlong reddish-brown curls, even the sprinkling of freckles across his cheeks taking on a rosy glow. He'd noticed this pretty young woman several times since the New Year long weekend.

Often enough to conclude she must have taken up residence in The Crossing.

Often enough to begin scheming how to get up close and personal.

The child constantly at her side had been all that held him back from approaching her. Married women were way off limits to his way of thinking. He ran a nervous hand through his hair, then impulsively offered it to her.

"Couldn't just stand there and watch your kiddie get hit. Joey Lambert, Ma'am. Glad I could be of service."

The blue eyes skittered away from his, as if the cracks in the pavement were more interesting. Straight white teeth bit her bottom lip, as the young woman hesitated briefly before taking Joey's hand.

So long he wondered indignantly if she thought the contact might contaminate her.

As she shook hands, she flashed a quick upward glance, smiling politely with none of the radiance of her first smile.

"Sienna Smith. Pleased to meet you Joseph. And this is my daughter, Gwyneth Smith."

She gave the girl a gentle nudge to remind her of her manners.

"Thank you for saving me, Mr Lambert."

"You've got pretty names, you and your Mum." Self-conscious with hero status, Joey sought to change the subject.

"Do you think so? Grandma says when your name is Smith, you need something a bit different to 'stinguish it from all the other Smiths."

Interestedly noting the inference that 'Smith' was the woman's maiden name, Joey was sufficiently curious to fish for more information. Renewed hope flared in his breast thinking she might be available after all.

"Do you live here in Oxley Crossing, Gwynna?" Questioning the child was a risk that had Joey holding his breath. Especially when out of the corner of his eye, he saw Sienna frown at her daughter; but when she made no move to put a stop to the conversation, he breathed a little easier.

"Yes, Mr Lambert." Gwyneth was as free with her smiles as Sienna was parsimonious. "Mummy's a teacher. She's going to start work as soon as the holidays are over."

Joey's heart sank again.

'Teacher' meant a university education. From time to time he'd flirted unsuccessfully with other young teachers doing their country service in The Crossing. He did an honest day's work for an honest day's pay, and found it offensive when a pretty girl talked down to him as if a mere yard hand at the sawmill was beneath her. As if his lack of education meant he lacked intelligence.

With a pack of younger siblings, his parents couldn't afford to send him to uni, and he'd taken the best job he could get. But, ever the optimist, he thought maybe this girl was different. Maybe she'd realise he wasn't stupid.

He'd see.

"Mummy, can I go and get my ball, now? I can see it in the gutter across the road." Gwyneth interrupted his musings.

"I'll get it," Joey volunteered, then, returning, ball in hand, he pushed his luck a little.

"How about joining me for a coffee at Tan's?" He gestured to the bakery-café beside them.

This time it was Sienna, eyes cast down to the pavement again, who blushed.

Shy?

Joey's eyes opened wide. He hadn't realised shy girls still existed. He was used to the girls he'd grown up with, who were all as assertive as the blokes. His pulse rate accelerated slightly.

"I'd like to Joseph. I really would." Sienna flashed him another of those split-second smiles, then lowered her eyes again. "I've got an appointment to get my hair trimmed. I'll be late if I don't get going."

"Say hello to Thea and the girls for me. Can we take a raincheck on the coffee?"

Thea and the girls?

Was this unassuming young man really a wolf in sheep's clothing? A momentary panic almost sent her fleeing until she recalled how much she owed him.

"That would be good. Bye Joseph, and thanks again for saving my girl." She gave a little wave and, taking Gwyneth's hand, quickly disappeared round the corner.

"Bye Mr Lambert," Gwyneth called. "Thanks for bringing my ball back."

Joey stood staring after them for a moment, then giving himself a mental shake, headed off in the opposite direction, back to the tiny flat he rented behind Bill Whitman's place. He'd pulled a swifty there, beating out a couple of other blokes looking for accommodation. The idea of continuing to share the sleepout at the farm with his younger brothers had been incentive enough to urge him to approach Hazel Whitman as soon as Robert won the election and moved to Canberra, vacating the flat behind his parents' house.

Whistling as he walked, he pulled up in front of the library. Nodding to himself, he pushed open the door and strolled in.

"Hi Aunt Eddie," he called, following the greeting up with a smacking kiss on the lips. Edith Patterson, the librarian, blushed and tittered.

"You and your nonsense, Joey Lambert," she bridled. "How can I help you?"

"With what you're best at, Eddie. Advice and information. With all the recent layoffs up at the mill, I've been thinking it'd be a wise move to look for another job. Maybe acquire a few decent qualifications along the way."

"Wonderful, Joey. I told you years ago that's what you ought to do."

"You did. I listened, and here I am Aunt Eddie." She wasn't really his aunt, but she'd taken him under her wing a long time ago when he'd been the victim of the school bully, and ever since she'd been his honorary aunt.

"Then let's go into my office and discuss your options over a coffee. Sue," she called to her assistant, "hold the fort for me, Dear."

Continued…….

Lena West

About the Author

Born in tropical North Queensland, Lena loves living close to the sea, although she moved frequently during her early years, living everywhere from Capital cities to isolated farms. Her most recent home has a deck overlooking the sea, which is her favourite room in the house, although, when the local birds come to visit, it is often hard to retreat to the computer and write!

After working as a primary school teacher in both her native Queensland, and later in New South Wales where she met her own romantic hero, she took a very early retirement to travel Australia with him, in a motorhome. This idyllic lifestyle lasted several years, during which she took the first steps towards fulfilling her lifelong ambition to write.

Storytelling came naturally - she had been making up stories for her own entertainment all her life, but it wasn't until she began traveling that she had time to write down some of her favourites. Now a self-published author, *Marrying Alan Morgan*, is the first in a series of rural romances set in the fictional town of Oxley Crossing. She also writes standalone contemporary romances and Australian historical romances.

She has an addiction to happily-ever-afters, in both her reading and her own stories, so the romance genre was a natural fit, and the variety of places she has lived have all added to the settings in which she brings love to life.

You can find Lena on Facebook at:

https://www.facebook.com/LenaWestAuthor/

or sign up for her newsletter at:

www.lenawestauthor.com

Other Books by

Lena West

Historical Romances

 **Unto Death** https://www.amazon.com/dp/B07D3MZ1L4

 **Emily's baby** https://www.amazon.com/dp/B07TPDN13W

Contemporary Romances

 **Loving Fenella** https://www.amazon.com/dp/B07B3RLS98/

Contemporary Series

Love in Oxley Crossing Series

 **Marrying Alan Morgan**

https://www.amazon.com/dp/B0774V1L25/

 **Saving Jonathon Armitage**

https://www.amazon.com/dp/B0788GCQJQ

 **Finding Mr Wright**

https://www.amazon.com/dp/B07C98B7PJ

 **Electing Robert Whitman**

https://www.amazon.com/dp/B07KWKLJG6

 **Redeeming Josh Marten**

https://www.amazon.com/dp/B07RNHBYG7

The Wyldeflower Series

(Coming soon)

Connect with Lena!

Be the first to know about it when Lena's next book is released!

Sign up to Lena's newsletter at

www.lenawestauthor.com